MW01077515

HUE & CRY

Elizabeth Yates

Edited by Gloria Repp

Bob Jones University Press, Greenville, South Carolina 29614

Library of Congress Cataloging-in-Publication Data

Yates, Elizabeth, 1905-
  Hue & Cry / by Elizabeth Yates : edited by Gloria Repp.

    Summary: Jared Austin, staunch member of the mutual protection
  society that defends his 1830s New Hampshire community against
  thieves, tries to temper justice with mercy when his deaf daughter Melody
  befriends a young Irish immigrant who has stolen a horse.
    ISBN 0-89084-536-0
    [1. Deaf–Fiction. 2. Physically handicapped–Fiction. 3. Robbers and
  outlaws–Fiction. 4. Emigration and immigration–Fiction. 5. New Hamp-
  shire-Fiction.] I. Repp, Gloria, 1941- II. Title. III. Title: Hue & Cry.
  PZ7.y213Hu 1991
  [Fic]–dc20
                                                          90-19147
                                                               CIP
                                                                AC

HUE & CRY

Project Editor
  Wanda Sutton

Cover and illustrations
  Stephanie True

©1953 Elizabeth Yates
©1991 Bob Jones University Press
Greenville, South Carolina 29614

20 19 18 17 16 15 14 13 12 11 10 9 8 7

Publisher's Note

In the early years of the nineteenth century, mutual protection societies against robbers and horse thieves were organized in many New England communities. The Hue and Cry was such an organization, serving the towns and villages of eastern New Hampshire, including the fictitious town in which Jared and Jennet Austin lived. Committed to uphold law and order, Jared and his sons, Rufus and Benoni, are enthusiastic members of the local Hue and Cry Society.

Jared and Jennet have lived a peaceful life for many years. But when their daughter, Melody, befriends Danny O'Dare and the horse he has stolen, Jared Austin finds that he must draw upon all his reserves of faith and wisdom in his desire to temper justice with mercy. His problem is compounded by the fact that Melody is deaf. He has taught her to read and write, but he fears that she is still just a child in the deeper things of the heart. On the other hand, young Danny, an Irish immigrant, is already well acquainted with hardship and disappointment, but he is in danger of growing embittered. *Hue & Cry* is a story of tenderness and courage, of far-seeing faith, and of sacrifice richly rewarded.

Books for Young People by Elizabeth Yates

Chapter One

Melody Austin sat by the hearth, carding wool. Every few minutes she looked up at her mother; but Jennet, at the loom in a corner of the kitchen, was absorbed in her weaving. Melody watched her mother singing to herself as she moved the shuttle and worked the treadles. Jennet Austin was a plump, comfortable woman with brown hair turning gray, and she had the look of one whose years had been well spent in practical pursuits.

Finally Melody saw her mother glance up at the clock on the mantel. She knew then that it was time to start preparations for the evening meal. It was her task to bring in the water for her mother's needs; so she put down her carding tools and picked up a pail that was standing near. She left the room and went out the open door to the well that stood a few paces from the house.

She swung the long sweep from its balance on a pile of stones until it hung over the well; then she lowered the bucket until she felt it touch the water. It dipped and bobbled as it tilted to the water, the strain on the pole increasing as the bucket filled slowly. When Melody felt that it was full enough, she put her weight against the pole and drew the bucket slowly up and onto the ground, poured the water into her pail, and swung the sweep back to its resting place.

Jennet was busy at the kitchen table. Melody put the pail down beside her and went out again. She went toward the well and leaned over its stone curbing.

There was a piece of sky at the bottom of the well, shimmering slightly since the water was still disturbed. Melody saw her face reflected in the piece of sky and smiled at the sight. The water-smile wriggled and rippled across the water-face, and the sight was so ludicrous that Melody's smile widened. Gradually the water became still and Melody's face began to look as it did when she saw herself in a mirror, but she had no liking for mirrors though she had a distinct affection for the piece of sky at the water level in the well. It was all hers, and it was always there. Even at night she had been able to find it, and the stars in it looked brighter than they did in the sky overhead.

The stones that lined the well were coated with moss, and water dripped from them. On one that jutted out from the others a frog was seated. Fixed, immovable except for an occasional blinking of an eye and pulsation in his throat, he gazed at Melody and Melody gazed at him.

"Pong–" croaked the frog. The salutation echoed in the damp, dripping hollow of the well, and its reverberations made a series of overlapping sounds.

Melody shaped her lips and leaned over the curbing, trying to return the guttural greeting with a sound of her own making.

The frog blinked.

Melody leaned farther over the curbing. There was a dull thudding coming up from the bottom of the well. She watched the water forming into drops that splashed from the stones, but it was not coming from the water. It was deep down and heavy, as if it were coming from the earth. She straightened up quickly, ran a few paces from the well, then flattened herself on the ground, placing one ear hard to the grass. She heard the same rhythmic reverberations coming through the earth, only they were clearer now, more meaningful. She listened long enough to assure herself that it was the hoof-beats of a horse traveling distantly at a hard pace, then to assure herself of the direction in which he was going—whether toward her, or away.

She got to her feet and ran across the field to where a granite boulder stood, from whose height she could catch a glimpse of the road before it rounded the bend. If she could climb up to the top of the boulder in time, she could see whose horse it was. Breathing hard from her race across the field, she pushed back her long brown braids and threw herself against the boulder, digging her fingers into familiar crannies and reaching for toeholds with her bare feet.

She had no way of knowing whether she would reach her view-place in time but, half hauling herself and half climbing, she gained the top. Below her and beyond her father's fields lay the road, a hundred yards of unobstructed view. She looked north, for the sound she had heard told her that the horse was running south. She put her hands to her eyes to shield them from the light that she might see better in the space of vision the open road gave her.

A horse appeared, streaking over the road. The rider, pressing speed hard, was leaning low over the horse's neck. Melody smiled with the pleasure of recognition. It was Mr. Turnbull's bay mare from the farm three miles up the road. Melody could not mistake the fine head with its wide white flash between the eyes and the long full tail. She lifted her hand to wave; then she dropped her hand quickly and crouched on the rock so that she would not be seen. That was not Mr. Turnbull, though it was his mare. Whoever was riding it must have been in great urgency or he would not have been pressing the animal so, beating the mare's flanks with a switch even while she was going as fast as her four strong legs could take her.

Melody slid down off the rock and ran along a narrow path that skirted a brook. She had to tell Rufus and Benoni about this. She turned into a small piece of woodland and raced through it to the edge of an open field where her brothers were bundling corn. Melody ran up a hillock and stood still, breathing deeply to recover her breath. Then she neighed like a horse. It was a deep sound that cut the silence like the teeth of a saw on a smooth length of wood.

Rufus looked over at the team hitched to the wagon, but the heads of both horses were drooped. He looked behind him and saw his sister waving to him from the hillock.

"Ben," he shouted to his brother, "there's Melody!"

They watched her.

Melody lifted her hands above her head and clapped them vigorously. The sound she made was like the sound of a horse galloping hard on a hard road. She put her hands on one of her brown braids and swung it against herself; then she brought her two hands together and pointed south.

Rufus interpreted her signals. "Someone's bay mare is racing toward the turnpike."

The boys dropped what they were doing and went to the wagon. Quickly they unharnessed the horses and led them away.

"If we take the short cut through the woods, we may be able to head him off," Benoni said, as he tightened bridle straps.

In less than a minute, the speckled roan and the heavy black were cantering along the edge of the field. Rufus and Benoni leaned low on their horses' necks, gripping with their knees.

Melody watched her brothers disappear into the woods. She smiled and waved, though neither one of them saw the gesture. She did not understand why her brothers always wanted to know when she saw a horse being ridden hard by a rider she could not identify, but she delighted in informing them. It was one of the things she could do, and it needed little explanation, for it was so quickly swallowed up in action.

An hour later Melody was seated with her parents at the supper table. Jennet put food on their plates and then gave a sigh of annoyance as she covered the heavy iron pot, standing it near the coals on the hearth to await the return of Rufus and Benoni.

"Melody says they're on the chase again," Jennet explained to Jared, "and who knows when they'll be back? I'll keep their meal hot, but I wish they were here to have it with us instead of racing all over the country."

Jared gave the blessing as if all the members of his family were present. "We thank Thee, Lord, for this food and for all Thy providing. May it help us to grow strong in Thy service. Amen."

Melody lifted her bowed head and smiled swiftly across the table at her father. Jared reached out and put his hand on hers. His gray eyes met her blue eyes in a glance of love and understanding: better than any words to Jared, meaning as much as words to Melody.

"I wonder whose horse it is this time," Jared remarked.

"Melody says it's Mr. Turnbull's bay mare."

"Stolen for the second time this summer!" Jared exclaimed. He shook his head. "That's almost too fine a horse for a farming man to own.

"There'll be small reward, if any, from Mr. Turnbull, for he's like all of us farm folk. We may have potatoes in our cellars and hay in our barns, but we've no money in our pockets. Now, if it had been this horse they were chasing–" Jared reached into his pocket and took out a carefully folded paper "–it would be worth their while." He chuckled. "That is if they caught up with the thief."

Jared unfolded the paper and smoothed it out on the table. It was a handbill such as was printed in hundreds and posted in stores and inns for the apprehension of horse thieves. Embellished with a galloping horse and large letters designed to catch the eye, it advertised a generous reward.

ONE HUNDRED DOLLARS REWARD

for the return of

BLUE LIGHTNING

a handsome gray stallion belonging to
Captain Isaac Mallow
of
Portsmouth, New Hampshire

This horse is a fine stud, brought from Tripoli three years ago. He has already sired more than a dozen colts, and his progeny are noted for their spirit, stamina, and endurance.

BLUE LIGHTNING was last seen in his pasture on the afternoon of August third. Hoofprints leading away from the pasture indicate that the thief was headed west.

MEMBERS OF THE HUE AND CRY AND ALL HONEST MEN TAKE NOTICE: WHOEVER APPREHENDS THIS THIEF AND SECURES HIM IN ANY GAOL OF THE UNITED STATES SHALL RECEIVE THE REWARD.

TAKE NOTICE also that any information regarding the location of the thief will be rewarded
by
Arnold Thompson
and
Jonathan Bartlett
The Hue and Cry Society of Portsmouth
New Hampshire
The fifth day of August, 1836

N.B. PRINTERS THROUGHOUT THE UNITED STATES:
You are requested to insert this notice in your papers for HUMANITY'S SAKE. Let the thief be brought to Justice! Let a noble horse be returned to his rightful owner!

Melody bent over the handbill. She was more interested in the drawing of the horse than in the lengthy words, many of which she did not understand. She shook her head, and her long braids swung back and forth like pendulums. She had not seen an unknown gray horse that afternoon, but a familiar bay who belonged to a neighboring farmer.

Jennet took the paper in her hands and read it. "If Rufus could only catch up with the thief, he would have the money he needs to go West." She looked across the table at Jared.

"Do you want him to go?"

"No, I do not," she answered stoutly, "but he wants to go so much, Jared. He'll never be happy here. These fields are too small for him. He's restless. He wants to be free."

"That's what all the young are wanting."

"There's nothing wrong in it, is there?" Jennet flashed back.

Jared smiled. "Would you like to go West too, with Rufus? To the rich stone-free land in York State or the Ohio Territory?"

Jennet leaned toward him across the table. The gleam from the lamp catching in her eyes and lighting her hair made her look like a young and eager girl. Melody gazed anxiously from her mother to her father.

"Oh, Jared, if we could–if only we all could go! Life must be so much easier out there."

"I have a notion life is the same wherever you live it," Jared said slowly.

"But everyone says it is easier out there!"

"You mean everyone hopes it is," he reminded her. "When they get there, I expect they find that it's the same round of work."

"None of them come back to tell us differently."

"No, because they've made homes there and worked the land. A man stays where he's done that, no matter how hard the work is. It's the rootless young who are always pushing on to new worlds. Rufus has the horizon before him, but this is our land, Jennet, and we've put our best into it for nearly twenty years."

Jennet looked away wistfully. "The tales you hear of the new lands make you think heaven might have touched hands with the earth–rich soil to work and the winter winds less chilling."

"But a man's fields must still be marked; and if there are no stones to use for walls, there'll be hard work splitting timber into rails for fences. And weather is always a question mark. If the winter winds are less cold, the summers may be more hot. We'll be content where we are. Let the young break the crust of the new soil."

Jennet shook her head as if to shake away a dream. "I won't leave you, Jared; and I know you won't leave New Hampshire."

Melody looked up suddenly as if she were aware of something cutting across the quiet of the room in which they were gathered. Jared and Jennet turned to the girl, seeing the familiar listening look on her face. Melody brought her hands together and made with them the sound of a trotting horse. She pointed to her two brothers' empty places at the table. She got up from her seat on the bench and ran from the room.

"I'm glad they're back so soon," Jennet said. "I don't like it when they're out all night."

"If Rufus is old enough to go West, he's old enough to be out all night," Jared commented.

Jennet nodded. "Rufus may be, for he's passed eighteen this summer, but Benoni is only a boy, and I like to know where he is."

"A boy of sixteen is almost a man."

Jennet gave no heed to his remark, but went to the hearth to give the stew a stir. Rufus and Benoni would be in soon, and they would be hungry.

Melody stood in the doorway of the house, waiting for her brothers. When she saw them start from the barn, she ran to meet them. Rufus held out his arms and she leaped into them. She was a lightly built girl, and he swung her up level with his head and then above it. She might have been a child for the ease with which he handled her. Setting her down again on the ground, he kissed her on both cheeks.

Melody smiled. Then they had been successful in what they had done, and Mr. Turnbull's mare was probably grazing peacefully in her own pasture, for only Pepper and Midnight were loose in the barnyard, dipping their noses into the watering trough and shaking their heads as they satisfied their thirst.

Melody followed her brothers into the house and sat down at the table to go on with her interrupted meal.

"That wasn't such a long chase," Jared said.

"No, we caught up with him at the ford," Rufus answered. "He'd stopped to water the mare. Think of it, after he'd been running her so!"

"When we got there," Benoni went on, "he had just started to stain that white streak down her head with some hickory juice. But we would have known that mare even if he had dyed her all over."

The boys gave themselves heartily to the generous plates of food Jennet set down before them, and for a few moments no one asked them any questions.

"Where is the horse now?" Jared broke the silence when Jennet took Rufus's plate to put more food on it.

"We led her back to her own barn and told Mr. Turnbull to keep a better eye on her in the future."

"And the thief?" Jennet asked.

"We left him at the sheriff's house as we rode through the village," Rufus answered briefly.

Benoni kept his eyes on his plate. He had a tender heart, and he had begged his brother to let the thief go; but Rufus, angered less by the deed than by the welts rising on the mare's hide from the lashes she had received to press her speed, had refused.

"He was just a lad," Rufus explained, "one of those Irish immigrants they bring over to work in the mills. He'd started from Lowell this morning, and Mr. Turnbull's mare was the third he had used today. Beating the life out of one fine animal after another!" Rufus exclaimed as his voice grew thick and his face darkened with anger. "I'd like to have given him a horsewhipping."

Jared looked across the table at his eldest son. "Work in the mills has probably been beating the life out of him; that's why he had to try to escape."

"What do they come here for then?" Rufus burst out angrily. "Why don't they stay in Ireland?"

Jared kept his eyes on his son. "That remark comes strange from one who has set his heart on going West."

Melody went to the hearth and brought a platter of corn-cake to pass to her brothers.

Rufus took a piece, then flung his arms around his sister and held her close to him, resting his head on her shoulder for a moment.

Melody smiled, more to herself than to him and brushed her lips against his cheek.

When she approached Benoni, he put his arms around her too. It was a hasty, impulsive gesture, but it conveyed what was in his heart.

Jared, his eating done, went on speaking slowly. "Last week, when I was painting the stencils for Seth Rollins's house up Stoddard way, a traveling man came by and Mrs. Rollins asked him to share the noon meal with us. He had come from Eastern Massachusetts, and when the talk swung to the subject of the mills, he told us there was such a world-wide demand for cotton that the mill owners could answer it only as they could get more and more hands to operate their looms. But it was the cheapest labor they were interested in, for only that would keep the price of cotton down."

"The cheapest labor?" Jennet asked. "What would that be?"

"Irish immigrants," Jared answered. "They write letters to the different townships in Ireland. They send broadsheets to be posted in public places, and on them they tell of the wonders of America–of the work waiting for the unskilled, and the good pay."

"But you said it was the cheapest labor!"

Jared nodded. "They tell them noble things about the land and induce them to come, especially the restless and the idealistic; then they load them into ships and treat them little better than cattle. When they land them on our wharves, the foremen from the mills are there waiting to claim them. The foremen tell them what the pay is and hold it before them, and the currency, because it is new to them, looks as if it would buy the world." Jared shook his head slowly, helplessly.

"Is their lot such a sorry one?" Jennet queried.

"Perhaps not, but they come here young and strong and full of dreams. The work soon drains their youth away, and the rough treatment they receive makes them bitter."

"Once they're working they've got a good life, haven't they?"

"A good life? Fifteen hours a day and a wage of fifty cents."

"When you were a boy, you got only fifty cents a week."

"True, but I was learning my trade. Mr. Toppan gave me the wisdom of his years and the skill of his craft so that they might give me my own work in time."

"You often work more than fifteen hours a day even now."

"Sunrise to sunset, that's a farmer's life and a journeyman stenciler's too, but I'm thinking it's a different kind of day than that spent between the walls of a building with machines clacking around you!"

"How is it that the lads and the girls are so willing to leave their land?" Rufus asked.

"They've had famine there for some years past, and life has not been easy. Any new way can look better than the old, when the old has been hard."

"I wish we'd let the boy go and not taken him to the sheriff," Benoni muttered. "I liked the sound the words had as they slipped over his tongue, and the look in his eyes was the look of a dog that had been beaten."

Jared stole a sympathetic glance at the younger of his two sons. "Were it not that horse-thieving were an evil in itself, I could wish the lad had got beyond your reach–but by his own legs, not the legs of William Turnbull's mare."

"At least you might have brought him here for a good meal before you turned him over to the sheriff," Jennet said reprovingly. "He might have stood up better to the law with something in his stomach."

"What's become of the corn you were bundling?" Jared asked.

The boys looked from one to the other.

"It's up in the high field still!"

"And so is the wagon with the ears of corn in it!"

"There's a moon tonight that will help you bring the wagon down to the barn," Jared said. "It would do our cows and pigs no good next winter if the wild creatures of the forest thought you'd spread a feast for them."

The boys pushed their bench away from the table and got up from it.

"Is everything set for the husking tomorrow night, Father?" Benoni asked.

Jared nodded. "Everybody around here knows you want them to come. I saw Tip Ferris today, and he says he and his fiddle are all ready."

"If we've a husking bee on tomorrow night, then Melody should get to bed," Jennet said. "We'll be cooking from sunrise on to get enough ready for hungry folk. Go along with your brother, Benoni, and see that the corn is safely housed."

As the boys were leaving the room, Jared brought the handbill from his pocket and called to them. Rufus took it and opened it, placing it on the table near the lamp. Both boys read it slowly.

"One hundred dollars reward!" Rufus said over and over again, his eyes gleaming. He knew better than anyone else how he could use such a sum.

"We'd have to turn him over to the sheriff to get the reward," Benoni murmured, "no matter how beguiling he might be!"

"So you would," Jared commented.

"And so you should!" Jennet exclaimed.

"If you catch up with him," Jared said, looking at Jennet, "bring him here for a good meal before you turn him over to the sheriff. I'd like him to know there's kindness in the land as well as justice."

Rufus and Benoni left the room. Melody and Jennet cleared the table and washed the dishes while Jared took down the Bible from the small cupboard over the fireplace and sat down to read from it. When Melody had finished her work, she settled herself on the floor beside her father, put her arms around his knees and looked up into his face, watching his eyes as they traveled across the page and his lips as they shaped the words he was reading aloud.

Jennet, her work done, stood by the hearth and gazed at them. They looked more like brother and sister, she thought, than father and daughter, for Jared was still thin and reedy, and though his sandy hair had grayed with the years, his face was unlined. Jennet heard Jared come to the end of his reading. From custom she bowed her head while he prayed. His words were intimate and conversant, as if God were within the range of his voice. One by one he said their names, asking God's blessing on them all.

"Night after night you do this, Jared," Jennet said sadly, "but it's done Melody no good."

"I do not ask that the child's ears be unstopped," Jared replied, looking up at his wife, "but that she will have a good life."

Melody had leaned her head against her father's knee. Her eyes were closed. There was a smile on her face.

"She's fast growing to be a woman," Jennet said, "and there's only one life for a woman. That life won't be for Melody, for who will ever want to marry her?"

"God has been good to us, Jennet. He will be good to Melody."

Jennet drew her breath in sharply. "Jared, let her do as I wish. Let her go into the cotton factory in Manchester and learn a trade as you did when you were a lad. There'll be no one to take care of her when we're gone, but at least she'll know how to work."

Jared did not move. To have put his arms around Melody as he longed to do would have alarmed her. She was happy in his presence. She was quiet with the words from the Bible that she had taken into her mind.

"Rufus and Benoni would care for her if we weren't here," Jared said in a voice that was little more than a whisper. "There may be someone of her own later."

"But Rufus wants to go West, and Benoni wants to be a painter as soon as his hands have the skill."

Melody stirred and opened her eyes. She looked first at Jared, then turned to her mother. A line of wondering wrinkled her brow. She understood the love in her father's eyes, but she was disturbed by the expression on her mother's face.

Jared stroked the girl's brown head, but he kept his gaze fastened on Jennet. "You've always been the practical one. Perhaps you are right."

"At least she wouldn't hear the noise of the reels," Jennet said, "and her fingers are as clever as any child's, and you've taught her to read and write; so they could write out on paper what they expected her to do."

"I've taught her to draw pictures too," Jared reminded her. "Why shouldn't she find her living in making beautiful things for people the way Benoni will?"

"You said only the other day that people didn't want beautiful things any more, that all they wanted were cheap things." Jennet took a few steps toward Melody. Leaning over, she tapped the girl on the shoulder; then she turned and started from the room.

Jared kissed his daughter good night. Melody rose to her feet and followed her mother silently from the room.

In the unfinished loft above, where much of the space was used for storage, Melody had her bed. After she had undressed and slipped into it, Jennet sat down on the edge of the bed with a small bottle in her hands. Melody shook her head at sight of the bottle, but she turned obediently on the pillow while Jennet poured a few drops of the liquid into one ear, then into the other.

Jennet stood for a moment by the girl's bed and held the bottle up to the window. It was almost empty. She would have to make more before the summer came to an end so that she would have a supply for the winter. The moon was bright, bright enough for her to see the writing on the label.

REMEDY FOR DEAFNESS. TAKE THE GARDEN DAISY ROOTS AND MAKE JUICE THEREOF. LAY THE WORST SIDE OF THE HEAD ON THE PILLOW AND PUT 3 OR 4 DROPS INTO THE BETTER EAR. DO AGAIN FOR 3 OR 4 DAYS.

Jennet read the words as if she would find in them the healing that the medication itself had not given.

When she returned the bottle to the fireplace cupboard, Jared looked up at her from the book that was still open on his knees. He saw the anguish in her usually placid face, and the reproach.

"Who is to say which way is the better?" he said gently. "You've been putting daisy juice in her ears since she was a year old, and I've been praying for her."

They could hear the boys returning from their work, going upstairs quietly to their room.

Jared shoveled warm ash over the big log at the back of the hearth so that the coals would keep until morning. Jennet crossed the room to turn back the covers on the bed that filled the corner opposite her loom.

Chapter Two

By sunrise the members of the Austin family were about their tasks. Jared had saddled his horse soon after breakfast and ridden off to finish painting the flowers he was stenciling on the walls of a house in a nearby village. Rufus and Benoni had returned to the high field to collect more ears and bundle the stalks of corn. Jennet was busy in the kitchen. Melody had gone to the pasture to bring the three cows in for milking.

Melody stood by the bars of the gate and opened her mouth. "Moo-oo." The low, guttural sound echoed across the dewy morning. "Moo-oo." The sound came stronger the second time.

The cows raised their heads. One of them mooed in response. All three came slowly toward the bars. Melody fondled each one and rested her face in turn against the long, smooth-coated heads. She twisted her hands around the curved horns; then she let down the bars and the cows walked solemnly into the barn. Melody put her milking stool and pail beside the first one, and with skillful, tender fingers she drew out the milk. She smiled as she worked, crooning to the cows, trying with her lips the shapes of new sounds. Every now and then she placed her ear against a strong, smooth neck to hear the low rumbling that was a cow's conversation with her.

When they were all milked, she turned them out to the pasture again and carried the milk to the house. Then, with a basket over her arm, she climbed up into the haymow to search for eggs. One of the hens was still laying. At the sight of her, Melody stood still. The hen opened her beak and made a series of sharp little clucks. Melody bent nearer to her.

"T-t-t." She pressed her tongue against her upper front teeth, breathing out lightly.

The hen blinked.

Pleased that her greeting had been acknowledged, Melody put her hand to her mouth and made the sound again, enjoying the feeling of her breath on her upheld fingertips.

Out in the barnyard she saw the rooster flap up onto the edge of a water barrel. He moved his wings and threw back his head, opening his beak wide.

Melody watched him. She knew that he was greeting the morning with some sound, but it was beyond her range and she could not catch it to answer him back. The smile that had been on her face faded. She looked up in the air at a family of swallows perched on the barn roof. She could see the vibrations of their throats and she longed to know what the sound was that they were making so that she could make it with them. On her way to the house with the eggs, she stopped by the well and leaned over the curbing to observe her frog.

There he sat, immovable but for the pulsations in his throat.

Melody opened her mouth and forced out a sound that traveled down into the watery world.

"Pung–" the frog answered.

Melody smiled. There was someone who understood her, who could return her greeting.

She saw herself in the piece of sky at the bottom of the well, the piece that belonged to herself alone. The sky looked lighter when she smiled. She wanted to remember that, when the ache pressed around her heart and made her not want to smile. The quivering piece of water deep down in the well had an odd look to it if she didn't smile. It looked empty. Empty things were lonely, and Melody knew more than she wanted to about loneliness. She went to the house with the eggs and placed them on the table at which her mother was shaping dough into loaves.

Melody stood before Jennet and held out both hands to her, looking up expectantly.

"Oh, there's plenty for you to do!" Jennet exclaimed, pointing to a basket of apples on the floor.

Melody nodded. Picking up a knife from the table, she carried the basket of apples over to the low stool by the hearth.

She started to pare them carefully, beginning at the blossom end and curling around and around until the skin came off in a long thin piece. When Jennet was busy putting her loaves into the oven, Melody tossed a paring over her shoulder to discover who her true love would be. She looked at it quickly, not wanting her mother to see what she was doing. The paring had fallen clumsily but unmistakably into the shape of a letter *D*. Melody snatched it up again and went on with her work.

Whenever Jennet left the room or her back was turned, Melody threw a paring over her shoulder. It fell so often into the letter *D* that she began to smile at it when she picked it up. She wondered what sound the letter *D* made so that she could make it when her true love came to claim her. She wondered where he would come from. He would be tall and strong like Rufus, but his heart would be tender like Benoni's. When she tried to see him in her mind's eye, she could see only someone who was as like her father as two seeds in an apple were alike, someone whose hands rested gently on her head and whose lips moved so carefully that she could see the words on them.

Jennet glanced around the kitchen. She was pleased at the sight of the work that was in hand. Her loaves were baking in the oven. Apples had been sliced into pastry shells and would go into the oven when the bread came out. Bowls of custard stood cooling by the open window. She had pressed enough cider for a township, but for those who preferred perry, there was still that to be made. She clapped her hands to get Melody's attention; then she pointed to the basket of pears that Rufus had set inside the door earlier that morning.

Melody nodded. She knew what her mother expected of her. She was glad to have something else to do.

Jennet set out the sugar and spice required for the perry. She watched Melody start her work; then she left the room and went toward the barn.

Rufus was busy sweeping the barn floor. Jennet watched him, proud of this first son of hers whose shoulders were broad and whose arms were powerful. He had been a sturdy baby, and his birth had been an easy one. Rufus had been born a year after she had come from her home on the other side of the mountain to marry Jared and live in the house Corban Cristy had built. She had been glad it was Jared she had married, though it was Corban she would have married had he not despaired of the weather and lost patience with the stubborn land. In hot impatience he had gone West, leaving his land to Jared and his house to Jennet. So they had been married, and the love they had known when they were children lived again.

Jared was light of body, but he was strong in spirit, and he had made the land yield enough for them to live on. During the winters when the land was at rest, he had traveled over the country following his own bent of decorating the inner walls of houses. Since he was often away for a week at a time, it was good company for her when the first baby came. Rufus had grown quickly. At only a few years of age he was helping his father; by the time he was twelve he was doing most of the work on the farm, and Jared was free to ply his trade as a journeyman stenciler all seasons of the year. But Rufus would not be with them much longer. He had already given his heart to young Martha Dunklee, and his mind was set on going West.

When Rufus was two years old, Benoni had come into the world. From the first he was a tender child, and his grasp on life had not been strong. It had taken all Jennet's skill and care that first winter to keep the boy with them, but once he had started growing he had grown well. He had early learned to help with the tasks of the farm, but his heart was never in the land. It was in following the work his father did, the slow quiet work of bringing beauty where plainness was. But while it was walls that delighted Jared, it was furniture that pleased Benoni. Painting patterns on chair backs and clock faces called for deft hands and an imaginative mind, and Benoni had these at his command as much as he had his gentle ways and easy humor.

Jennet would have been glad to welcome six more sons, but the only other child that had come was the little girl. She had puckered her face into something resembling a smile almost as soon as she was born, and the smile had taken her into her father's heart. Jared had sat on the hearth holding the baby in his arms while Eliza Dunklee cared for Jennet and made her comfortable again.

"Is the child all right?" Jennet had asked, for it seemed strange to have a new member in the household and so little sound of her presence.

"Yes," Eliza said, "she's going to be no trouble, that small one."

"She's so quiet," Jennet fretted.

Then Jared spoke from his seat by the hearth. "She's making melody in her heart."

And so she had named herself, for they had never called her by any other name.

Jennet, watching Rufus's strong arms and rhythmic gestures as he swept the barn floor, took such joy in him that she stood silently. It was not until he stopped that she came forward into the barn. Rufus smiled. "Listen," he said, "do you hear what I hear?"

They stood together in the doorway. The August sun was warm about them. The air was rich with the feeling of late summer fruitage. Birds were gathering, preparing to migrate. In the silence an apple could be heard falling from a tree with a dull thud. But there was another sound, far off, but coming nearer, the clicking of cloven hoofs and the heavy turning of wheels.

"I hear the roll of a wagon and the tread of oxen," Jennet said.

Rufus nodded. "Someone is on the way."

Together they stood in the doorway of the barn, Rufus leaning against the side post and Jennet her arms akimbo, her hair tossed by the breeze, and eagerness in her eyes. Their faces were turned toward the bend in the road. A Conestoga wagon came into sight, its white canvas top gleaming like a sail full-bellied with wind. Two heavy-boned oxen were drawing it, their ponderous gait half as slow as a man could walk. On the seat of the wagon was a man. Beside him sat a woman with a baby on her lap. They were young, but there were three other children in the back of the wagon, peering out at the sight of a house and barn.

In the wagon was piled all the furniture they could take and all the equipment they needed to establish themselves–a plow rubbed shoulders with a bedstead; a tall clock wrapped in a quilt was secure between ladder-back chairs. The wagon drew nearer. The woman smiled and lifted her arm to wave, and the children, seeing Jennet and Rufus, waved gaily to them; but the man never took his eyes from the road before him. As the broadside of the wagon passed by, the words written on it became visible:

WE'RE BOUND FOR OHIO

Jennet and Rufus turned their heads and watched the wagon rolling slowly down the road until a bend took the great white sail from sight and left only small swirls of dust which soon settled into the road again.

Jennet put her apron to her eyes. Something in the woman's face had touched a spring within her. "She'll never give herself wholly to Ohio, for there's something of her heart she's leaving in New Hampshire," Jennet said aloud. Perhaps it was the grave of a little one, she thought, and her heart went around the bend of the road to the woman. Pack up everything in a house that you could, take the setting hen and her eggs and slips from the lilacs, but there was one thing you could not take and that was the heaped earth marking a grave.

"He's bound for the new land," Rufus said enviously.

"He is," Jennet said with a nod, "and he's going to let himself see nothing else but the stone-free fields and the rich loam he's heard so much about."

Rufus started whistling between his teeth.

Jennet turned toward him. "You'd like to follow that wagon, wouldn't you?"

"I would indeed," Rufus said; then he stretched his arms out before him and bent them back again as if to feel the ripple of their strength through his whole being.

Jennet watched him admiringly.

"As soon as I have the money to buy a wagon and a pair of oxen, I'll be on my way."

"Not alone?" she teased.

"Oh no," he said with a laugh, "but I'm not asking Martha to marry me until I know we can start out life in the new territory."

"Since Martha's brothers went West, she's all the help John and Eliza have until the little ones are grown," Jennet commented.

"I know that, but I know, too, that they'll not hold her back when I have the right to ask for her hand."

Jennet was proud of Rufus and the clear way he saw ahead for his life. "I wish I had the money to give it to you."

He laughed good-naturedly. "Folks like us have everything but money. However, I've got a swift-running horse, and I'll catch up with a thief one day and claim the reward. Then I'll have something to jingle in my pockets!"

"There's a hundred dollar reward posted now."

Rufus flashed a smile at his mother. "Blue Lightning?" He lowered his voice as if he were exchanging private information. "I've a feeling that I'm going to get that horse sometime, and that time may be soon."

Jennet, suddenly conscious that they were both idling their time and that it was not yet noon, said abruptly, "You might use your horse to advantage and ride around to the neighbors' houses and remind them to come to the husking tonight."

"I'll do that," Rufus responded. "The barn is all ready. Did you ever see such a pile of corn?"

"Never!"

"That's the best land we have, that high field. It always yields a good crop."

"It was corn from that land that fed the countryside in the starvation year," Jennet said reverently, remembering the terrible winter and spring of 1816 when crops had frozen again and again, and hundreds of New Englanders had gone hungry. With an effort she returned to the present. "Where's Benoni?" she asked.

"Still up there. He'll be down when he has the stalks all bundled." Rufus started toward the stall where Midnight was tied. "When shall I tell the neighbors to come?"

"Tell them to come at candlelighting time, and the more of them the better," Jennet replied. "I've pies and tarts and loaves of gingerbread, and cider enough for the county."

By late afternoon, preparations for the husking bee had been completed, and the final chores of the day had been attended to. The cows had been milked and sent back to pasture. The horses had been turned out in the field so that their stalls might be free to accommodate some of the neighbors' horses. Jennet had changed from her day dress to the one that was for all occasions next to Sundays. She had brushed Melody's long hair and braided it neatly; then she and Melody left the kitchen so that Jared and the boys might wash themselves in the big tub and put on fresh clothes. At half-past five they sat down together at the supper table, and Jared asked the blessing.

"That we may grow strong in your service, Lord, and that all who come here tonight may be blessed by our home–not the invited guests alone, but the wayfaring man if such there be. Let it not be said of this household that it gives of its heart only to those it knows, but let it be always an impartial giver as Thou art, Lord, sending Thy rain upon the just and the unjust. Amen."

"Amen," the family gathered at the table murmured in response.

While Jennet was ladling soup from the iron pot, Jared took a paper from his pocket and started to open it.

"Another handbill?" Jennet asked.

Jared nodded.

"Another stolen horse?" Rufus asked eagerly.

"No," Jared shook his head. "This tells of a school for the deaf in the state of Connecticut."

"A school!" Rufus exclaimed.

Benoni leaned toward his father. "You mean there is a place where Melody could go and learn like other children?"

"Apparently," Jared said slowly. "I'd just finished my work in Duncan Ames's house when a stranger came along and we all sat down to noon meal together. We started talking about our families, and when I spoke of Melody his face lit up as if you'd set a candle by it. 'Oh,' he exclaimed, 'there's a school in Hartford where they are teaching the deaf!' We talked more, and he gave me this handbill to read about it."

"Does it cost money?" Rufus asked.

"Yes. A hundred dollars a year."

Jennet sat down at the table. "You've taught her to read and write, Jared. She reads the Bible for herself now. What more could she learn at a school?"

"She might learn to speak."

"To speak! But the child's tongue is tied so she can't speak."

"Sign language, Jennet. They would teach her to use her hands more meaningfully than she does. And it's said that they are even teaching some of the deaf to make sounds."

Jennet looked at her daughter. Rufus and Benoni turned to Melody, and Jared gazed her way. Melody felt their concern and stared at them with puzzled eyes. A slow rise of color mounted into her cheeks. What had she left undone, she wondered. Why were they all looking at her? She turned to Jared, her face troubled and questioning. He put down his spoon and placed his hand on his heart; then he reached across the table and laid his hand lightly against Melody's heart. It was the sign they had between them that all was well. Melody understood the gesture, and the questioning look eased from her face.

"What more would they teach her than you have already?" Benoni asked eagerly.

"The world of learning would be open to her," Jared said, "and it would not be only for Melody to take more into her mind, but by the language of signs she would learn to communicate with others. She might in time express her own thoughts."

"But she does that now," Jennet said.

"Yes," Jared agreed, "clumsily, with the movements of her body. At the school she could be taught to use her hands as ably as we use our tongues."

"It's mysterious," Rufus said.

"It's magical," Jennet added reluctantly.

Jared smiled. "It's neither one. It's the principle and practice of a whole new theory."

"But the money–" Rufus began.

"Even if we had it, Rufus," Jennet said, "I wouldn't want her to go."

"Jennet!"

"Mother!"

She shook her head. "The Lord made her the way she is for a purpose. I'll not have anyone tampering with His work."

A startled silence came over the table. Melody was oblivious of it as she read the sheet of paper that her father had placed before her. Meaning more to her than the promise of education was the information it gave that there were others in the world like herself. She had thought she was the only one. "I am not alone," she said to herself, and there was deep comfort in the words.

Rufus and Benoni ate hurriedly. Soon they got up from their bench and went to the barn to light the lanterns and make immediate preparations for the arrival of the neighbors.

Jared looked across the table at Jennet. "Everything we do is in some small way improving on what we have in this world. We improve the land so its yield will be greater, our horses so they will be swifter, plain walls in houses so there will be more beauty, and all the time we are working with the Creator. Shall we stop our work at a dumb child?"

Jennet shook her head. There was a confused and frightened look in her face. "People say that God has laid His hand on Melody."

"A hand of love, not of limitation."

"They say that I have done some wrong, and this is my penalty."

"Should it be Melody's too?"

"They say–" Jennet began.

"Do they say these things to you?"

"No. They whisper them behind my back, but I know. It is on their faces when I see them, when they look at Melody and turn away from her. Pity they could have, but they do not. They are fearful of what might happen to them if they look too long on the Devil's–"

Jared motioned Jennet to silence. He turned to Melody quickly and shaped a barn with his hands, then pointed to theirs.

Melody placed her hands across her chest and raised her eyes in questioning.

"Yes. Go," Jared said.

Melody left the table and went to join her brothers.

"Let us not talk this way before the child," Jared said sternly. "Something in her knows, even though she may not hear our words. Jennet, her hold on happiness is such a slippery one; if she thought we had lost faith in her, life would be hard indeed."

"She's happy enough," Jennet said stubbornly.

"Yes. She smiles, I know. She has since she was born. But have you ever heard her laugh? I haven't."

Jennet looked at Jared and for a moment her face had the bewildered, questioning look that was so often seen in her daughter's.

"Jennet, you believed in me once when people said hard things about me in that starvation year. How is it that it is so difficult for you to believe in your daughter?"

Jennet dropped her gaze and her voice was husky when she answered, "Perhaps because she is bone of my bone and flesh of my flesh."

Jared left his bench and came around the table. He stood beside Jennet and put his hands on her shoulders. "But she is heart of my heart, Jennet, and something of us both went into her."

"So we are responsible," Jennet burst out. "That is what irks me so. Sometimes the very sight of the child reminds me of my sins."

"We are responsible to do all we can to prepare her way for life," Jared said quietly. "More than that no parent can do. Melody did not come into the world with empty hands. No one does."

Jennet swung around to face her husband. Her eyes were flashing. "Let her work in the mill then; that will busy her hands."

"No. Not until she is older. Not until we have tried–"

"But the money! There's not that much in this household, nor ever has been or will be!" Jennet said hotly.

"Perhaps not tonight, or next week, but she couldn't go to school until next month." He smiled and drew Jennet toward him. "We'll stand aside and see the Lord work. He has ways none of us can fathom, and we'll follow one of them when it appears."

"But–but how will we know His way?"

"I can't tell you that now, Jennet. All I know is that when it comes, it will be like the shining of the sun on a bright morning, and everything will be clear." Jared raised his head. "The neighbors are coming!"

"Oh, Jared, the husking bee! I'd almost forgotten about it and here I've worked since dawn to get ready for it. What a man you are to make a woman forget her tasks!" she chided.

"Go now and welcome our neighbors and get them started with the husking," Jared urged.

Jennet smiled. She fluttered her hands through her hair and smoothed them down her dress. She stood a-tiptoe to kiss Jared, then spun around and ran from the room.

Jared watched her from the window. There was little light left in the sky, but it was enough to show the swirl of her dress as she went across the grass, running out of the twilight and into the barn. He turned back to the table. Slowly he picked up the dishes and took them to the big pan standing on the hearth, but before he began his housewifely task, he moved the slip of paper lying on the table toward the lamp and read it again carefully.

It must be a beautiful place, he thought, the American Asylum at Hartford; beautiful not because it was set on a hill and commanded a wide view of surrounding country, but because of the good things that were done there. He glanced away from the paper and across the room with its gathering shadows. It was not hard for him to see in his imagination, as he so often saw the designs he would put on a bare wall, a room full of boys and girls with slates in their hands. But they were learning more than the writing of words. They were learning to use natural signs of language that would open the way to communication with their fellows.

He thought of all he had not been able to teach Melody, particularly of his utter helplessness when it came to explaining to her wrongdoing of any kind. Right she knew instinctively, but its opposite was something he had not been able to make her comprehend.

He turned back to the piece of paper on the table. Yes, if she were to be a useful member of society, she would have to receive more education than she could gain at home, and though there was small hope that she would ever be able to give the proper sound to words, at least her capacities for understanding could be unfolded. Best of all, she would be drawn out of her solitariness.

"Terms and Conditions." Jared read the heading of the last column of print. "The Asylum will provide for each pupil: board, lodging, and washing; the continual superintendence of health, conduct, manners, and morals; fuel, candles, stationery, and other incidental expenses of the schoolroom; for which, including Tuition, there will be an annual charge of one hundred dollars."

Jared's eyes traveled down the column until he came to the last paragraph. "Each person applying for admission must not be under Ten, nor over Thirty years of age; of good natural intellect; capable of forming and joining letters with a pen legibly and correctly; free from any immoralities of conduct, and from any contagious disease. He should be well clothed; that is, in general, he should have both winter and summer clothing enough to last one year."

Jared looked away from the words, away from the shadow-filled room and into the glow cast by the lamp. The expression on his face was that of one who had a quiet assurance within him. So often he could not see the way, but always he could be sure that there was a way. He folded the paper. Opening the door of the fireplace cupboard that held their treasures and their hopes, he took down the Bible and slipped the paper between its pages. Then he returned the book to its place, closed the little door, and set himself to washing their supper dishes.

When he had finished, he blew out the lamp and picked up one of the pewter candlesticks arranged on the mantel. Bending down, he lit a taper at the fire and touched it to the candle's wick. His eyes roamed the room; then he leaned over and blew out the candle. There was no need to leave it burning on the table and so give invitation to the house when it was the barn that held people, music, and feasting. The wayfaring man, if such there should be, could join them in the barn. Jared turned his back on the hearth with its coals banked by a mound of ash and walked away from the house, leaving it to the darkness and itself.

Jared paused at the threshold of the barn. A score of people were sitting in a sea of shucks, while baskets of golden ears of corn rimmed the sea like the shores of a promised land. Beyond the baskets were trestle tables spread with food, and Tip Ferris was leaning against one of the posts, tuning his fiddle.

A shout went up from the people busily husking corn. "A red ear! Melody's got a red ear!"

Jared stood in the doorway, and his heart went out to his daughter. A red ear gave her the right to kiss the lad of her choice or, if her courage failed, to be kissed by every man there.

"No, no, not Melody!" Jared exclaimed, but his words were lost in the shouting and reckless cheer that always attended the discovery of a red ear.

Melody, sitting deep in corn husks, had been so busy and so oblivious to the life around her that she had forgotten her dread of finding a red ear. Now she held it before her, and a look of terror came over her face. She swung the ear above her head, hoping Rufus or Benoni would see it and come to kiss her; but they were busy shoveling the husks into a heap. A lanky boy started edging through the crowd toward Melody, and the girl got to her feet unsteadily. He was not to her taste, but she knew if she did not use her privilege of choice she would make herself the target of every boy and man in the barn. She looked frantically around her and saw her father standing in the doorway. With a low whimper like a frightened animal she ran toward him, wading through the shucks, jumping over the baskets of corn, and skillfully avoiding the outstretched arms of the merrymakers who were trying to catch her and claim her for a kiss.

Jared felt the whirlwind force of her arms around him and the press of her warm lips on his own as the passion of her love was intensified by her fear. For a moment he held her tightly, while friends and neighbors laughed good-naturedly at the sight. Then he released her, and she gave him a swift kiss of gratitude and ran out into the night. He watched her go, losing her in the darkness somewhere between the house and the barn. He thought to follow her and then decided to leave her alone.

Melody ran toward the house. She was hot and there was a throbbing in her head. To cool herself and quiet the anguish that invariably rose within her when she was in a crowd of people, she crawled into a fern brake near the well and pressed herself against the earth. The ground was cool, and there was dew on the ferns already. She could feel their caress. Slowly the freshness of the night and the deep peace of her retreat eased the aching within her, and she felt her own peace come over her again. She could part the ferns when she wanted to and through them get a glimpse of the open barn door, the figures of the merrymakers, and the flickering shadows cast by the lanterns. Above her the moon, risen by an hour, was filtering pale light through the ferns. She lay curled in her familiar position, one ear to the ground, eyes half-closed as if on the edge of sleep.

From far away a faint reverberation came through the ground. Melody stiffened and pressed her ear closer to the earth, closing her hand over her other ear. It was a horse. She knew that. Perhaps someone was coming late to the husking. But the gait was unusual. It was not even and certain; it was halting. She changed her position to get the sound more clearly. The horse was lame. Her face clouded. Melody could not bear to think of an animal hurt and unable to speak of its suffering. It was no one coming to the husking bee, for who would want to ride a lame horse?

As the sound came more distinctly, she caught another sound interwoven with it and almost of a piece with it but lighter. It was the tread of a person walking beside the horse. Scarcely daring to breathe, Melody pushed the ferns aside and eased her body along the ground to catch a glimpse of whoever might be going down the road at such an hour.

Then she saw them–a gray horse limping badly, and a tall, thin boy walking close beside the horse with his head turned inwards as if they were talking together. They stopped a few feet from the fern brake, and Melody's heart beat so hard that it started the throbbing in her head again. She saw the tall figure of the boy look around him–at the house in darkness, at the barn full of light, at the horses tied along the fence rail, nickering softly at the gray who was standing in the road.

The boy left the horse and crept like a shadow nearer the well as if to assure himself of his safety; then he raised the well sweep and lowered the bucket into the water, bringing it up full. He carried the bucket to the horse in the road, who drank long and thirstily. After that, he drew another bucket and quenched his own thirst.

Melody could not see the boy while he was drawing water, but the horse was within a few feet of her and she gazed at him. He was handsomer than any horse she had ever seen– light of leg bone yet deep across the chest, dappled gray with a silver and black tail that almost swept the ground, and a silver mane that reflected the moonlight. The horse held one of his back legs just above the ground. Melody could see that it was swollen near the ankle and must have pained him, for the muscles above the swelling twitched frequently.

Then Melody felt her body tensing. This was not any horse. This was Blue Lightning, the horse that the whole countryside was seeking, the one for whom a reward had been posted in every township. She watched more closely, recalling the description on the handbill. She was impatient for the boy to start down the road with the horse so that she could run to the barn and tell her brothers. They would over-take the lame horse and the walking lad in little time. She smiled as she thought of the pleasure they would have in the chase.

The boy must have felt safe, knowing that the people from miles around were gathered in the barn, for he took his time with the water. Then he picked up two or three fallen apples from a nearby tree and gave one to the horse, putting the others in his pocket. He bent down to move his hand over the swollen hock, rubbing it as if he would rub away the pain. He was so near the fern brake that Melody could have touched him had she wanted to stretch out her hand.

When he straightened up again, she saw his face, pale in the moonlight. She caught her breath in her throat for she thought he must be seeing her too, so near they were. She did not feel afraid of him, only afraid that he would discover her presence and so know that he had not been alone. She kept her eyes on his face as long as it was in the moonlight. It was a thin face, crowned with a mat of heavy black hair. There was fear in it and a look of hungering, but there was kindness in it too, and there was tenderness in the way his hand ran knowingly over the horse.

The boy turned toward the horse and Melody could see his lips moving. Placing his hands on the dappled neck, he made the horse turn around, and together they started up the road; not past the barn with its wide open doors, but back over the way they had come. Melody put her ear to the ground and followed their slow course, hoping to determine the direction they would take at the crossroads. As she listened, it seemed as if the horse used his leg more comfortably after the rest and the water.

She slid backward out of the fern brake and stood up, shaking herself; then she went toward the well and leaned over it. There was a patch of moonlight on the water, and the face that looked back at her was a pale face with wide open eyes, a face not unlike that of the boy's except that it was not crowned, as was his, with a heavy mat of hair. She knew then that she would not tell her brothers about Blue Lightning. This time she could not set in motion the Hue and Cry. If she did, she would have been giving something of herself away.

Melody went to the house and up the stairs to her loft bedroom. The moon had made a white place on her bed, and she sat on it as if it were a magic carpet. It would move. It would not stay there long, but as long as it was there she would live in her dream. The moon shone kindly into the loft, resting on the oak chest that held her clothes, on the shelf Benoni had made for her books and slate, on the apples strung from the beams for drying, and on her father's go-to-meeting boots that six days of the week hung from a rafter with beans in them to keep their shape and on the seventh day responded to his feet.

Melody sat still. Slowly the moon moved across the sky, away from the window, and the square of light was there no more. Melody put her head in her hands to hold the tears that had come into her eyes. She knew what loneliness was, but never before had she known such yearning as she felt then. Like so much in her life, it was nothing she could put into words; but her heart was drawn out after a lad with a thin, pale face and a haunted look in his eyes.

Chapter Three

The following Sunday after church, the men found it difficult to talk about the pastor's sermon with the more urgent business they had on their minds. From all over the immediate countryside there had come reports that Blue Lightning had been seen. Some children had watched him being ridden hard down the turnpike, but as their father was plowing in a distant field with the family horse, there was no one at hand to give chase. One of the villages to the north reported that a gray horse had gone through it at noon on Friday at a thundering gallop, so fast that the men standing on the steps of the general store could not decide among themselves what the rider was like and no one was certain which road at the crossroads had been taken.

The Hue and Cry, assembling quickly, had sent men down every road, but in an hour's riding overtook no one. Travelers on the roads had been queried, tollgate keepers had been questioned, but no one could give reliable information on the direction the horse had taken. Appearing and disappearing, the gray seemed as able to evade searching eyes as pursuing hoofs. Yet the sheriff could take his oath on having seen such a horse and the members of the Hue and Cry, who supplemented the law because their horses could outrun the sheriff's, knew they had not been summoned to pursue a phantom.

There were some who had been as aware of the rider as they were of the horse, but their stories differed, and listening to them all, it was impossible to determine what sort of man could ride a horse so daringly and elude his pursuers so skillfully. Old Granny Swallow, who had been too infirm to go to the husking bee at the Austin farm, was the only one who seemed able to give any kind of description of both horse and rider. She had been sitting by her window on the Friday evening, alone in the house, and she had seen a dappled gray horse with a magnificent tail and mane being led down the road. She had described the rider, then walking beside his mount, as little more than a boy, and she had thought nothing of the two of them, assuming they were late goers to the husking.

It was after church that Granny told what she had seen, but the men gathered on the steps were inclined to smile at her words, for Granny was known to see things when she wanted to be part of the conversation.

"That was me you saw on my way to the husking bee," Moses Trimble said with a laugh.

"And were your own legs so strong that you tired them out beforehand by walking beside your horse?" Granny asked tartly. "This man was walking," she insisted.

The men smiled tolerantly, thinking that Granny's eyes were getting too old to be trusted. Young Peter Swallow winked at them, then put his stalwart arms under his grandmother and carried her out to the waiting farm wagon.

Pastor Wilson joined the group. On most Sunday mornings he would have rebuked his people for discussing matters other than the sermon, but a horse lover himself, he was as interested in the chase as the rest of them. "It's been more than a week since the thief rode out of Portsmouth on Blue Lightning, and if he's got no farther than this countryside, something is holding him up," he commented. "Either he's fearful to cross into Vermont where they say the horses are faster though they've never proved it; or he's in hiding, saving the horse for a dash one night; or–"

The men looked intently at Wilson, their expressions more alive than they had been during his sermon.

"Or what?" the question rose from them.

"Or he's ridden the stallion so hard that he's worn it out or broken its wind."

"Then it'll be good for nothing if we recover it," Rufus Austin said impatiently.

Pastor Wilson shook his head. "That may not be the case." He looked at them challengingly. "Men, let's find the thief and restore the horse to his owner. Could we do the Lord's work better today?"

"No!" they shouted.

"No!" Deacon Phillips bellowed in a voice louder than all the men put together.

Wilson looked pleased. "So be it. There'll be no sermon this afternoon, but we'll meet here at two o'clock, every man on his best horse. We'll cover the roads of this township and search every hiding place. Are you willing, Deacon Phillips?"

"I am."

"And you—Jared Austin, John Dunklee, Moses Trimble, William Turnbull?" One by one he challenged the men of the town.

A roar of approval went up from the gathered crowd.

"We'll find the thief and bring him to justice. We'll return the stallion to his owner," Deacon Phillips called out. "New Hampshire men can defend their own honor."

"And their horses!" Moses Trimble shouted.

"The reward, Pastor Wilson, will it go to the man who finds the thief?" Rufus Austin's voice rose above the others.

The Pastor looked at him. "If one man helps another and we all aid the whole, the reward will be divided among us all."

The men nodded in agreement. Some of them turned and started away from the church steps to join their waiting families.

"We ride, then, at two o'clock!" Pastor Wilson called after their retreating figures.

"At two o'clock!" they shouted back zestfully.

With most of them it was the chase that mattered and the honorable activity of running down a horse thief; the money was incidental. Talking together, beginning to plan their strategy, they left the church to join the women and children waiting patiently in wagons and carriages, or to mount their own horses and ride off to their homes.

Jared got up on the seat beside Jennet. Melody had been lying with her head in her mother's lap and her eyes closed.

"Is the child tired?" Jared asked, as Rufus and Benoni climbed in and sat on the seat in the back.

"She's always this way on Sunday morning," Jennet said, an edge of impatience to her voice. "Her head hurts her."

Jared handed the reins to Jennet. "You drive and let Melody come to me."

Melody opened her eyes and smiled at the sight of her father; then she moved close to him and leaned her head against him. He stroked her head gently. If it held pain, he longed to ease it away; but if it was bewilderment that caused the pain, he knew not how he could reach it.

"It's hard for the child," Jared said, "sitting there for two hours on that wooden bench with no knowledge of what is going on around her."

Melody put her hand on the small slate that lay on the seat beside her. She took a chalk from her pocket and wrote carefully, "What were they talking about?"

Jared rubbed out her words and wrote, "A missing horse. Pastor Wilson and Deacon Phillips are leading the Hue and Cry in a search this afternoon."

Melody looked at her father, then raised her hand, pointed to the sky, and made a jagged line across it.

Jared nodded. "Yes. Blue Lightning."

Rufus leaned forward and put his hands on his sister's shoulders to get her attention. He pointed to her eyes, then to the sky and made the same jagged streak with his right hand.

Melody's eyes looked wide and startled. She shook her shoulders free from her brother's hold.

Benoni laughed easily. "Of course she hasn't seen him. She would have told us if she had."

"Yes, of course, she would." Rufus leaned back again.

Melody put her head down on her father's lap. She put her arms around his knees. Her grasp on him tightened.

He put one hand on her shoulder to assure her, the other on her head to soothe the pain that he could feel almost as acutely.

"You're coming with us, aren't you, Father?" Benoni asked.

"Yes, I'm coming."

"If we had a fourth horse, I'd be with you too," Jennet said.

The cart creaked on over the road. It was only two miles, but Jennet let the reins hang loose. She would not press the horses. They would have enough to do when they joined in the chase that afternoon.

The noon meal was soon over and the boys went to the barn to saddle Pepper and Midnight and Willow. Melody had seemed unusually remote ever since they had arrived home, sitting on her stool by the hearth and holding her head with her hands. Jared knew when there was something troubling her and he tried in every way he could to help her free herself. Shortly before he left, Melody came to him with her slate.

"If you find the horse will you bring the rider here?"

Jared read the words. He looked perplexed. If he alone found the gray and his rider, he would have brought them both home before he turned them over to the law, but if he found them while on the chase with the men of the township, he could not bring them home. Besides, he would not be riding alone. It would be his duty, as it would be the duty of every member of the Hue and Cry, to turn the rider over to the sheriff at once, and return the horse to his rightful owner, even if it meant riding to Portsmouth tomorrow.

He shook his head slowly and took the slate from Melody's hands. With unwilling fingers he started to write, "Blue Lightning's rider is a thief–" then he stopped and erased what he had written. "Thief" was a word he had not yet been able to explain to Melody and this was not the day to press her mind with word meanings. There had been enough to try her. He would not add to the day's burden. He shrugged his shoulders and smiled; then he looked at her for understanding. What he saw in her face startled him: no longer was there the look of the puzzled child but something of the woman whose life was in her heart.

He knew he could not leave her with the memory of uncertainty that shrugging shoulders implied, and something in her attitude challenged his own thoughts. This was an unusual thing they were doing, this summoning of the Hue and Cry on the Lord's Day. He had not been wholly in agreement with it from the start. He would make one request of Pastor Wilson and unless it was granted he would say that he and his two sons and three of the best horses in the township would withdraw from the chase. He would ask to shelter the thief that night before giving him to the law the next morning. The word of Jared Austin would be sufficient surety.

He picked up the slate and wrote one word on it, "Yes."

Melody flung her arms around her father. A sound like a bleat escaped her as she buried her head against him.

"What have you done to make the child so happy?" Jennet asked, coming into the room.

Jared smiled across the top of his daughter's brown head. "Only told her that if our search is rewarded the rider of the gray horse shall have the hospitality of our home for this one night."

"Oh, Jared!" There was reproach on Jennet's face. Fear flickered in her eyes.

"A hungry hunted man is not a dangerous man," Jared said quietly.

"You're always so sure." The reproach was still in Jennet's voice.

"Only of a few things." Jared freed himself from Melody's clasp; then he kissed Jennet good-by and prepared to leave.

Rufus and Benoni came up to the door with the horses and called to their father. Jared went out and mounted Pepper. Three hands waved; three horses turned.

"Wish us well," Rufus called over his shoulder.

"They'll not be back until they've found him, or until it's too dark to see," Jennet said to herself as the sound of their cantering hoofbeats fell away in the distance. She turned to look at the clock on the mantel. There were hours of the day before her, hours that should be spent reading the Bible; but first she thought she would try to do something for Melody's head.

She went to the cupboard by the fireplace and looked at her store of remedies. She put faith in them all, not so much because of the power resident in them but because using them meant that a step was being taken to relieve suffering, that something was being done, and to do something invariably eased Jennet's conscience.

She put her hand on a small box labeled "For the Headache." It contained a powder she had made early that summer when Jared had brought her some finely ground licorice. Following an old recipe, she had added to it a scruple of turpeth mineral and one of nutmeg, with a few drops of oil of rosemary; then she had let the mixture dry to a powder. The recipe had said it was wonderfully powerful when snuffed up the nose. This was her first opportunity to try it, and she was eager to see the effect it might have. She took the box in her hands and turned to face Melody with it, but the room was empty.

"Melody!" she exclaimed; then she clapped her hands loudly. She went upstairs to the loft, but Melody was not in her room. Quickly she ran to the window. Looking out, she was not surprised at what she saw. An exclamation of annoyance escaped her and then she nodded her head as if in understanding.

A figure in a blue dress, a small fleet figure growing smaller as the distance between her and the house grew greater, was running across the pasture toward the woods. Had Melody joined in the Hue and Cry too, Jennet wondered. No, she was only doing what any animal would do–taking her hurt into hiding. She would nurse herself in solitude under some tree in some secret place. There was a lake deep in the woods whose waters Melody loved. She might be searching it out for relief from the pain that had nagged her. Melody had done it before, Jennet knew; she would do it more often as she grew older and life pressed its strange bewilderments upon her.

Jennet, watching the girl disappear into the woods, felt an aching love for her. There seemed so much that she could never tell Melody, could never share with her; there was so much that she had to trust to nature to do for her. Jennet comforted herself with the thought that nature was a wise mother for all forms of life. The animals learned from her without words and Melody at least had words, though she could not utter them, and it was difficult to know how much of their meaning she grasped.

Melody had been a remarkably good baby, crying, gurgling, babbling to herself like all babies. It was not until she was well into her first year that they had any suspicion that there was something wrong with her. Only when she did not start to shape words as her brothers had, and, failing words, began to rely on gestures to make her wants known, did they begin to suspect she was different. "She does not hear," a neighbor had said one day to Jennet, and the words had seared themselves into Jennet's heart.

Jared had refused to believe that Melody could be different from other children, and he was determined to act with her always as if she could hear, but as the years passed it became more and more difficult. Rufus and Benoni used gestures with her as it was the quickest way to understanding, and Jennet soon began to rely on gestures too. Gradually, what voice Melody possessed lapsed into meaningless murmurings. To the gesturing of those around her, Melody responded with head, hands, eyes, and countenance. Her life became a living pantomime, amusing as the antics of a puppy, dainty and skillful except at times when, failing utterly to make herself understood, she relied upon passionate outbursts of behavior or withdrew into solitariness.

When she was five years old, Jared started teaching her all that it was possible for her to learn. Patiently he would shape words on his lips that he wrote on her slate. Tirelessly he would encourage her to shape words with her lips, though no sound came with them. He wanted her to have words to think with; words with which she could comprehend the thoughts of others; but no task he had undertaken in his whole life compared with the one that faced him then.

Melody learned to read and write, but no matter how Jared tried, he could not teach her to speak. The frog down the well had some means of communication with her, as did the horses and the cows; yet it was their speech they gave her and that was of small use to her in the world in which her life had to be lived. She had her own range of sounds–a whimper for fright or pain, a bleat like a lamb for happiness, a deep neigh like that of a horse for attention. Melody was aware that the sounds brought ridicule from all except her own family and a few understanding neighbors, and she preferred to dwell in silence.

Quite by chance, one day when Melody was still a baby in her cradle, Jared discovered her ability to respond to vibrations. The clapping of hands could arrest her attention, and subtler forms of clapping could convey a variety of sounds to her. When she began to toddle, he taught her to place one ear close to the earth and listen to the sounds that came through it. In time she could distinguish between vibrations of the different paces of a horse, of a cow walking slowly, or one of her brothers running across the grass.

The world was not so bleak as it might have seemed for Melody as she grew from childhood into little girlhood, and there was one agony she would never know which Jennet bore, sometimes in resignation, often in bitterness. When it began to be told throughout the countryside that the Austin baby was deaf and dumb, Jared and Jennet had been shunned by many of their townsfolk. People said it was a judgment upon them. Jennet would have despaired at times had it not been for Jared's steadfastness, which made little of the attitudes of others providing their own attitude was right. So they had lived their life during the week and gone to church on Sundays carrying the baby in their arms until she was old enough to walk and sit beside her brothers.

There were some who did not speak to the Austins from one year to another. It was hard on Jared, for he loved his daughter, and he was proud of the progress she was making against tremendous odds; and it was sad for Jennet, since she had given the child life. But the hearts of the townsfolk had begun to open, and rarely now was reproach made. Melody had grown up oblivious of the stern view some held of her, and the Austin family had grown more united because of it. Jennet could look back on the past with little anger and less resentment. It was not in her nature to attempt to look far into the future.

She turned away from the window and started from the room. Melody was safe in the woods, in the silence that was her element, among the creatures whose language she understood. She would not return until dusk, and then it would be to do her chores, bringing the cows through the pasture with her and into the barn for milking. Jennet was alone. She could do what she liked with the hours of the afternoon that lay before her.

She went downstairs to the fireplace cupboard and returned the headache powder to its place. Dutifully she put her hands on the Bible. She would read for a while, and the reading would make her sleepy, and no one would be there to chide her if she took a few hours sleep on the Lord's Day. But her hands slid over the Bible to the small volume of Mr. Whittier's poems that had just been published and that had been given to Jared a few weeks ago. She decided to read it and wait for Jared to read the Bible that evening to them all.

Her heart beating faster and her fingers tingling, she held the book of poems and sat down on the settle by the hearth. Her eyes glanced quickly at the clock. Now she felt there could not be hours enough left in the day for all she wanted to do. Far off on the turnpike she could hear the thudding of horses' hoofs and the shouts of men. They would find Blue Lightning if he was in their township.

Expectantly she opened the book. The sounds died away in the distance, and in the room only the low purring of the fire and the turning of pages aided the clock as it marked the passage of time.

When Melody reached the edge of the woods, she turned and gazed back for a moment, but there was nothing to draw her back. The house looked quiet under the strong heat of the sun; in the pasture the cows had sought the shade of a widespreading oak and were lying down, their knees tucked under them, their jaws gently moving; in the sky the swallows were wheeling airily. Everything in the visible part of her world was going about its own business, and Melody felt she could safely go about hers.

She leaned back against the furrowed bark of an ancient pine as she got her breath from her run across the pasture. The pine had been her friend on more than one occasion. She had climbed among its branches like a red squirrel. She had lain in its fragrant carpet of brown needles and watered them with her tears. She had clung to it in fright and desperation. She had dreamed with it as she lifted her head and looked at the sky through its branches. She had watched the branches move, gently swaying in the wind, and what she had been aware of was the tree speaking to her in a tongue she could understand. Melody stroked the rough bark in brief farewell. Today she would not stay long with the pine. She would go into the woods.

For a moment or two while standing by the tree, she had felt hesitant. Now she felt sure of her destination. High up the slope and deep in the woods was a spring-fed lake. Rarely on her flights from the household was there time for her to go there, but today she had as much time as there was light in the sky. There were no chores to do until evening and they were only the necessary ones since it was Sunday, and Sunday was a day of rest for people and creatures and the land.

A road led to the lake, a road that ran off the main road, but which was used so little that the grass was growing up in the middle and the forest growth was pressing in on the sides. The road had been traveled often enough three summers ago when the countryside had lain parched and panting under the hand of a drought. She had gone with her father and the wagon twice a day to the lake to bring water down in hogsheads and buckets for their own needs and the thirst of the stock. Nearby farmers had gone to the lake too, to draw water from it. The road had become as dusty and worn as any road in the county, but the level of the lake had not gone down by a span, though the brook that tumbled away from one side of the lake and over a rocky course to flow through Jared Austin's land had become a mere trickle.

No one went to the lake now except Melody, and she looked upon it as her own. Like the water in the well that mirrored the sky and gave her back her own image, the lake mirrored the sky and gave her back an image so much bigger that she could find no name for it. It was her secret place, her holy place. Her father had told her that everyone had such a place, a retreat from the world in which they talked with God.

Melody knew she could not talk with people, but she had no trouble talking with God. His voice she could hear, though the sound of words never came with it. Only when her heart was troubled and her head hurt so that she wanted to beat it against a tree was there such a void of silence that it was frightening. But the lake understood; for when winds ruffled it there was no image there, and when ice locked its waters and snow covered them there was only loneliness. The lake knew what times of waiting were. Melody had known many such times. She realized she would know many more as her life went on, but today was not one of them. This day of warmth and quiet would show the lake to be a smooth surface wherein the depth and beauty of the sky was reflected.

She pushed a low branch aside and came onto the woods road. She stopped short and a low sound escaped her lips. There were hoofprints in the earth. She bent over and traced one print then another with her fingers. A horse had gone up the road but it had not come down again. Had some member of the Hue and Cry thought to search the woods around the lake? Melody felt the curve of a print more carefully. The earth around it was not yielding. There was a slight crustation to it. These were not today's hoofprints. An uneasy feeling came over her, replaced soon by a small flood of anger. Someone else had discovered her secret world.

"No, no," she breathed inwardly, then stamped on the prints as if to erase their strange tiding. She would not share her lake with anyone else.

Turning around quickly, she ran back through the woods to the brook she had crossed a few moments ago. It led to the lake and she decided to follow it rather than the road. The ascent was not an easy one, but it was safe. There were boulders in the brook's course, huge boulders that would offer places for hiding should she discover someone at her lake or in the woods near it. She started up the brook, trying to persuade herself that the hoofprints might be one of her brother's horses; trying to convince herself that the heat of the sun had dried the tracks and made them tell a tale she had no heart to know.

Her father had taught her when in the woods to be as noiseless as a forest creature, to tread on her toes and find her way over ground that would not betray her, avoiding the rustle of leaves and crackle of twigs. From stone to stone she leaped, lightly and delightedly, soon forgetting her fear of what she might find in the brief venture up the course of the brook. The water rippled noisily over rough gray stones and silently over stones that had thick carpets of moss. In places, tall leaves of the wild iris marked the brook's borders; in others, jewelweed with its dainty orange flowers hung in graceful tangles. Here cardinal flowers bloomed and there a thick clump of alder promised a wealth of red berries.

She reached the turn where a great beech tree stood like a sentinel, its roots sprawling over the ground and reaching far down under the brook's bed. The water widened into a pool, and Melody laid herself flat on earth and moss to drink long and pleasurably. She lowered her face and let the water flow over it, washing the heat away. The brook divided here into several lesser streams, but Melody knew which one to follow. She clambered over the boulders and up the course over ground deep in leaf mold.

Noiseless as her approach was, her tread became even lighter and more cautious as the ground leveled and she drew near the opening in the trees which meant she had reached the lake. Swiftly she moved from tree to tree, feeling safe in the shelter of beech, birch, and pine until she reached a granite boulder that stood as wide as a house and half as high. She crouched low and crept around the boulder until she came to the edge of the water. Rough and sun-hot, the boulder was like a friend, giving back Melody's caress with one of its own. Cheered by it, she scrambled up on to it and sat looking across the water.

The lake was rippleless. A handful of clouds moving across the sky looked like cobwebs spun on the dark water.

The trees that bordered the lake were still. Melody flung out her arms and smiled. It was her world still, unclaimed and unmolested. The hoofprints on the woods road had been meaningless. She was safe from other eyes, delivered from the jangle of voices that filled the air with wearying vibration. Beginning at the rock, her eyes traveled around the shoreline that cupped the body of water in the green embrace of tall trees. Then she uttered a sudden sharp sound. Lying against a tree and not a stone's throw from where she was sitting was a saddle, a leather saddle. Her eyes scanned the shoreline and tried to pierce the forest green, but neither man nor horse could be seen.

She slipped down from the rock and made her way to the saddle. She put her hands on it. The underside was stained with sweat and there were short gray hairs in the leather, but it was not warm or moist as if it had just come off a horse. The outer side was a fine piece of workmanship, made without any joins as if a master saddler had done it. There was a bit of tooling around the edges and on one flap an initial letter had been burned into the leather: *D*. Melody ran her fingers around the letter, so intrigued by its design that she was unmindful of its mystery.

"*D* is for David," she said to herself, remembering a lesson she had had from her father with an alphabet book that went through the Christian names. On the opposite flap were the initials *O'D*. Melody traced them with her finger. *D* was also for Daniel, she thought to herself. There was a Daniel in the Bible about whom her father read to them sometimes, and she, leaning against his knees, followed the story with her eyes while the others had it from Jared's lips. That Daniel was a man greatly beloved; a man who had been told to be strong, yea, to be strong. But who was this Daniel? Melody put her head down on the saddle and smiled. Why should the *D* be for Daniel when the book had said *D* was for David?

She closed her eyes. The feel of the leather, the smell from the horse, the heat of the day, the quiet of the lake, all added up to give her an overwhelming sense of peace that washed over her like a tide. She curled her legs under her and wrapped her arms around the saddle, hugging it to her. At that moment there seemed no more reason to question its presence at the lake than to question the cardinal flowers growing along the brook.

Melody sighed happily. The smile that knew her well and that had given her her name rested as lightly on her face as the cobweb clouds on the surface of the water.

Chapter Four

A tall, thin boy walked slowly along the woods road, leading a gray horse. The horse was limping and the boy kept up a ceaseless conversation as if to comfort and encourage the animal.

"Sure and you'll be the better for the bit of exercise," he said, "but it's a measure of oats I wish I had for you. That would give you heart again, and we might be on our way tomorrow." He stopped by a blueberry bush and picked a handful of berries which he tossed into his mouth. "Oats for you and a bit of bread for me," he sighed, "bread that I could wash down with a cup of tea. But we'll be thankful for what we've got, eh, my laddie?" He rubbed his hand down the horse's head and took the flicking of ears as a response to his question.

He jerked lightly on the rope, and the horse got into his stride behind him, hoofs clicking on the stones in the overgrown road. When the lake was in sight, the boy led the horse to it and stood quietly while the horse drank; then he tethered the gray to a near tree and went over to the place where he had left his saddle. Whistling to himself and trampling along careless of sound, he came to a sudden stop, and his whistled tune was left in midair.

A girl was lying asleep, her arms half around his saddle and her head resting on it.

Danny O'Dare stood still and stared. Fearful of waking her, he caught his breath with an inward gasp and then closed his lips tightly. How had she got there when he had been on the only road leading to the lake and no one had passed him? Was there a house nearer than he had thought? But that was not possible. He had roamed the woods under cover of darkness to assure himself of the safety of his retreat. He wondered whether it was a ruse set to catch him and his only recourse was in leaving before she awoke and could give the alarm. He knew then that he must make his escape before she awoke, whether it was with his horse or without. But he would not go without his saddle; of that he was certain. He had brought it too far already to abandon it to a mere girl, and she a small thing at that.

He felt for the knife in his belt. He had done enough wrong the past week; a little more would hardly weigh on the scales, so heavy were they already. He would bind her hands with the length of rope he had with him and gag her while she slept. He would wait until darkness and make his escape then with his horse, even though the creature had no speed in him and but little strength.

Danny stepped nearer the girl, his eyes so intent on her that he did not see the twisted root which tripped him. He fell over it. "Oh, my sorrow!" he exclaimed as he disentangled himself.

The dry twigs crackled noisily, but the sound did not wake her. Danny stood up again and passed his hand over his eyes. It was they that were playing him tricks. She wasn't real. She would disappear in another moment and only his brown saddle would be lying there. It was too many wild berries he had been eating. Hunger did strange things to a man. If she was real, she would have wakened at the noise he had made when he tripped. He whistled again, shrilly, nervously, but the girl did not move. The smile on her face did not tremble. Her fingers, curled around the leather, did not shift. That settled it then. She was not real. She would vanish at his touch.

He approached her gingerly and, kneeling on one knee, reached out his hand to touch her. He held his hand in mid-air. Almost he did not want her to vanish into nothingness. He had been lonely this past week during which he had been fleeing justice; he had been lonely this past year in a new world of which he had heard so much and in which he had found only trouble. He reached out and touched her, then leaned back, half-expecting to see her disappear.

Melody shook her head and sat up. She turned her head quickly to see what had wakened her, and her eyes met the anxious gaze of a young lad who was kneeling on the moss not an arm's length from her. The wideness of her eyes and the flight of the smile that had marked her in sleep told of her surprise. She stared at the boy, trying to think why he was not strange to her. Then she remembered. She had seen him the night of the husking bee. She had watched him. She had shielded him. Oh, she knew him well, though he had not seen her before! Melody smiled and held out her hand to him.

Danny leaned back as if he were dodging a blow. She was real, and she was human. This was a trap. She had been sent there to spy on him. She would call for help. The woods might be full of armed men waiting to answer her call. Fear raged in him. He bent forward and grabbed her hand, twisting it so that the pain made Melody wince.

"Don't make a sound or I'll kill you," he whispered savagely, putting his other hand on the knife at his belt.

Melody shook her head and tried to draw her hand away.

"Where are they waiting for me?" Danny asked hoarsely. "How many? Are they mounted?"

Melody shook her head, pulling hard on her hand.

He dropped her hand and laid both of his on her shoulders. "Speak now," he commanded, "or I'll kill you sure."

Melody shook her head. There was no smile on her face, and the color had drained from her cheeks. The clutch of his fingers on her shoulders hurt her, but she was not afraid of him.

"Don't you mind if I kill you?" he demanded.

She shook her head.

"Come on, now," he said. "It's a trick, and you're all in it. You're all against me in this land. Tell me how I can get away, and I'll let you go."

She held her hands out before him, palms up.

He shook her violently; then his hands dropped from her shoulders and he got to his feet.

When Melody sensed that he had spent his annoyance, she put her hands up to smooth her hair, then reached into her pocket. But there was no chalk in it with which to write on a stone. She looked around her and pointed to a large white fungus growing on a tree.

Danny did not understand her silence, but he understood that she wanted the fungus. He went over to the tree and broke it off; then he brought it to her. Melody took it from him and pointed to his knife. Danny paused with his hand on the hilt. He did not want to be without defense, but whatever she had a mind to do, he knew that he could overpower her if he kept his eyes on her. Sure that it would not be hard to get his knife back again, he handed it to her. Melody smiled and nodded her head in a gesture of thanks.

With the fungus on her knees and the knife in her right hand, she started to carve letters in the spongy surface. Danny leaned back against a tree to watch her. Slowly the truth came over him and with it the reason why his whistling had not wakened her, nor his stumbling over the root. And now it was himself he wanted to kill, so angered was he. Melody's heavy brown hair fell on either side of her face as she leaned forward, intent on her writing. At last she looked up, handing the fungus and the knife to Danny.

"Who are you?" he read.

"Danny O'Dare," he printed on the fungus. "Who are you?"

"Melody Austin. Where do you come from?"

"Ireland," he wrote. "And you?"

"The farm at the bottom of the hill."

Her name and the place where she lived had been among the first lessons she had had from her father. Telling them, she had said all there was to say about herself. She stared at the fungus, then at Danny. Ireland was far across the sea. Her father had told her about it, but she had never thought to meet an Irishman.

"Where are you going?" she printed.

He had to search for a new fungus for his answer and while he was gone, Melody, looking around her, saw for the first time the gray horse tethered to a young beech. She went over and stood by him, putting her arms around the dappled neck. She whinnied softly, and the horse moved his head along her arm.

Danny held the fungus before her. "Anywhere."

"Is this Blue Lightning?" she wrote.

He looked startled, and the fear that had gone from his face came back to it again. How was it she knew the gray's name when he had not known it until a few days ago? Had she learned it the way he had, by seeing it on a handbill posted in a public place? He tossed the fungus aside as if tired of the game they had been playing. He took the knife from her hand and put it back in his belt.

Melody shrugged her shoulders; then she walked around the horse and felt the lame leg. There was a swelling that must go down before the horse could use his leg as he should. Her father would know what the trouble was. Her mother would know what remedy was needed. She picked up the fungus and took the knife from his belt.

"Come to my father's house with me."

"No," Danny said aloud.

She smiled and put her hand on her heart. Then she wrote, "I must go now but I will come back."

He seized the fungus. "Alone?"

She nodded.

"With food?"

She nodded and pointed first to the horse then to himself. She held her hands over her head and clapped them.

He held his high and clapped them, smiling questioningly.

She beamed at him, delighted that he understood the signal.

"Tell me again who you are?" she wrote. Then she tossed the fungus toward the lake, where it fell into the water with a smack. She stepped near him and placed her fingers gently on his throat.

Surprised at her gesture, then realizing its significance, he spoke slowly and distinctly, "I'm Danny O'Dare from County Donegal in Ireland."

She opened her mouth and a meaningless sound escaped her; then she placed her two hands against her heart for a moment and looked at him steadily.

He understood her and knew that she would not give him away.

She turned quickly and ran along the shore of the lake, dodging fallen branches, leaping from one rock to another. At a point of her own choosing, she swung away from the shore and toward the woods. She stopped for a moment and faced him, holding her hands high and clapping them ecstatically. Not until he answered her with a similar gesture did she disappear into the woods to follow the course of the brook.

The sun had not set behind the line of hills in the west when Melody came out of the woods at the place where the ancient pine stood. She was glad that she would have time to bring the cows in, do the milking, search out the eggs, and then slip into the house with her chores behind her. She had not been missed, she felt sure; she never was unless her tasks were undone. Approaching the house, she noticed that five or six horses were tied along the fence rail. Several members of the Hue and Cry had come back with her father and brothers, but she knew they had not brought any thief back with them. She smiled, thinking of the secret she carried within her. Only she knew the whereabouts of Blue Lightning and his rider. The Hue and Cry were no more likely to ask her to tell them anything than she was to reveal it.

After her tasks were done, she went to the oat bin and lifted the wooden lid. A mouse scurried across the slippery surface of the grain and dived through a hole in the corner of the bin. Melody squeaked a greeting, but the small creature bent on escape did not look back. She filled a measure with oats and tipped it into a bag kept in the barn for sowing; then she tied a string around the neck of the bag and hid it far down in the bin. Oats were precious and were fed carefully to the horses, but one of the guiding stars of the Austin family was that no hungry person should ever leave the house unfilled. Melody would not have been her father's daughter if she had not extended the precept to a lean boy and travel-weary horse sheltering on their land. She went to the house and slipped in quietly.

Jennet was the only woman in a room full of men, and she was caring for them well as she heaped their plates with food and filled their mugs with hot cider.

Melody moved through the room to the chair where her father was sitting. She knelt down on the floor beside him and put her head in his lap. He fondled her long brown hair with one hand. Melody felt happy in his recognition of her. She closed her eyes. She knew what had happened that afternoon with the Hue and Cry. For once it did not matter in the least that she could not hear them talking about their ride.

Deacon Phillips, who as well as being a mainstay of the church was the leader of the Hue and Cry that year, was shaking his head. "We've not failed to bring a thief to justice ever since our Society was formed twelve years ago, but the township has defeat to admit today."

"Are you sure you've searched everywhere?" Jennet asked.

The Deacon brought his hand down on the table. "We've covered every road in the township. We've searched every barn. We've followed every clue, and we're as near the end of our funds as we are of our wits."

Pastor Wilson sighed dolefully. He had thought they would be favored in their search on the Lord's Day, and he was more disappointed than the others at their lack of any measure of success.

"Vanished this one has," Rufus said. "We'll hear of him being brought to justice over in Vermont." Rufus did not feel the loss so keenly since he knew the reward would not have come to him in any case.

"I'm a New Hampshireman," the Deacon growled, "and it's the honor of our state I'm after. We've got as good horses and as able riders as any township in Vermont; yet we've let a thief elude us." He pushed his chair back from the table. "I'll bid you good evening, gentlemen. Come to my house tomorrow, and I'll reimburse you for the miles you've traveled. Good rest to you and to your horses."

The others followed him to the door.

"How far was it today?" Jennet asked when the men had left.

"The boys and I covered more than fifty miles between us," Jared said, "and Deacon Phillips directed us well, dividing us up so that every road was covered to the township's borders, and every likely trace pursued."

"Fifty miles!" Rufus exclaimed. "The pay for that will be just enough to put a new shoe on Midnight for the one he threw."

Jennet looked at him sympathetically, knowing that the vision he was pursuing had gone farther beyond the horizon.

"There'll be nothing for anyone in the way of reward for the next thief we apprehend," Jared said, "for the Society's funds are getting so low that any money received will have to go to building them up."

"The dues will help some."

"But they won't be coming in for another six months," Jared said.

"I don't care whether the funds are low or not," Rufus burst out. "The next thief I catch, I'll have every penny of the reward for myself."

Benoni sat on the floor beside his sister and took some jackstraws from his pocket to play with her. "It'll be winter before long," he reminded his brother, "and there's never much horse stealing then."

"Winter!" Jennet exclaimed, as if someone had mentioned the Devil.

Jared looked down at his two youngest. "Jackstraws on the Lord's Day," he said gently.

Benoni blushed and pocketed the sticks quickly. Melody looked at her father questioningly; then she got up and went to the fireplace cupboard. She had to stand on tiptoe to reach the Bible. Before she put it in her father's hands, she opened it to the place where she wanted him to read.

Jared smiled. "It's the sheep and the goats again," he explained as the others gathered around him to listen. He read the verses slowly. Melody kept her eyes on the page. " 'Inasmuch as ye have done it unto one of the least of these my brethren, ye have done it unto me.' " Jared closed the book. " 'Inasmuch,' " he said quietly. "That may be as meaningful as 'well done.' "

The boys soon left to go to bed. Jared banked the fire and blew out the lamp. The light of a candle was all that he and Jennet needed now. Melody went upstairs to her loft and Jennet soon followed her with the small bottle in her hands. Melody had drawn the coarse linen sheet up to her chin, but when Jennet came to stand beside her bed, she turned her head on the pillow obediently, willing to submit her ears to the nightly administration of daisy juice. Jennet bent over and kissed the girl; then she went downstairs again.

Melody reached for her slate that was on the floor. Taking it into bed with her, she prepared to count up to a hundred, marking off strokes with her chalk in groups of fives and adding her total when she approached the desired sum. Sure then that she had given her father and mother time enough to get into bed, she threw back the covers and sat up, fully dressed but for her shoes. She picked up her shoes from the floor and put them in the deep pocket of her dress. She groped her way to the oak chest and took from it a small square of linen which she used as a neckerchief. Then she knelt on the floor and put her eyes to a familiar crack. In the room below, the candle was still flickering, and its light penetrated the crack. When the light went out, Melody knew it would mean that her parents had gone to bed and would soon be asleep. She did not have to wait long for the light to go out; then she waited a little longer to assure herself that her parents were sleeping.

She left the loft and crept down the stairs, one step at a time, holding her breath and hoping no sound she could not hear would be heard by her parents and so draw attention to herself. She stood on the threshold of the big room where all their living was done and looked toward the bed in one corner. She could discern two forms, motionless under the heavy quilt. Walking on the tips of her toes so slowly and carefully that moments seemed like hours, she crossed the room to the bin near the hearth where the bread was kept. Lifting the lid, she reached in for a portion of a loaf, which she wrapped in her linen square. Creeping along the side of the room farthest from her parents, she went toward the door.

Her hand on the latch, she lifted it slowly so no scraping sound would be heard. She paused before opening the door. A squeaking hinge might arouse her father, and what would she say if he found her fully dressed with a half-loaf in her neckerchief? She stretched her arm up to the high hinge and rubbed her hand over it, back and forth, warming the iron. She did the same for the low hinge, then drew the door toward her and slipped out through a narrow opening. Breathing deeply, she brought the door shut again and eased the latch into place. She sat down on the doorstone and held her head in her hands to calm the turmoil within her. After a few moments, she took her shoes from her pocket and put them on. She went to the barn and got the bag of oats she had secreted; then she started towards the woods.

" 'Inasmuch.' " The word shaped itself in her mind and she wondered what the sound of it would be like.

The woods were speckled with moonlight and the water of the brook slipped over the rocks as if the stream were silver pouring from a mine in the heart of the hill. Melody climbed quickly up the way she knew well until she reached the lake. She lifted her hands above her head to clap and then thought otherwise. Approaching the clearing where the horse was tethered and where Danny had made his retreat, she saw him lying on the ground with his head pillowed on the saddle. He had taken off his coat to spread as a blanket over him and the moonlight gave him an added covering.

Melody placed the bag and the bundle near him. She reached out her hand to wake him and then thought better of her intent and withdrew her hand. Turning from him, she made her way down the course of the brook and across the fields to her home.

Chapter Five

For a week Melody took food to Danny and the horse. She did not go at the same time every day, nor did she always have with her oats and bread. Once she took some corn for Blue Lightning and an egg for Danny; another time she took him a small flask of milk. When it was possible for her to do so, she saved porridge from her morning meal, but it was difficult to hide and far from easy to carry, and she did not want to do anything that would cause her actions to be observed.

She did not understand why Danny would not make himself known, especially since Blue's leg got no better, and the swelling was moving from the hock and working up the leg. But there was so much else that she did not understand that this added no burden to her mind. She did what was expected of her around the house and farm, and in whatever portion of her time remained, she went to the woods. No one thought it unusual, for it had been her pattern of living for years past to go off by herself frequently.

She preferred to follow the course of the brook, rugged as it was, for then she left no telltale track in the long grass of the road. Her slate and chalk she now always carried with her, though there were times when there was no need for them. After the first day, Danny seemed determined to speak with her in words, as he spoke to Blue, and whether she responded or not made little difference with him. Blue did not reply in words to Danny's constant flow of conversation, but the boy never doubted that Blue understood him.

Melody was amazed at first and would often reach in haste for her slate; then she began to watch Danny's lips carefully. After another day or two she could begin to see the words on his lips as she saw them on her father's. Within her rose a longing to make the sounds that accompanied the words. It was as if Danny were calling to the voice in her, and the voice wanted to respond.

One day as they sat by the lake, a bird alighted on a near branch and watched them intently. That led Melody by means of gestures and slate to talk with Danny about birds. They found that they had a bird in common, one of the earliest arrivals in the spring. Melody saw the words on his lips.

"Cuckoo, cuckoo."

She smiled and clapped her hands, then tried to shape the name with her own lips, but no sound came. She wrote on her slate, "The Indians call him muck-a-wiss."

Danny looked at her. "You can say that."

The four words most often on his lips had become so familiar that Melody knew what he was saying. She shook her head.

"Try. 'Tis yourself must do it." He made the sound of *M* and placed Melody's fingers lightly on his nostrils in order that she might feel the sound as it came through his nose.

After a few moments she tried the sound herself. The effort was tremendous; and after she had made it, she sighed and folded her hands in her lap wearily.

Danny leaned back against the stone. "Sure and *M* is the easiest sound in the world to make," he said. "That's why all the most beautiful words begin with it." He went through a long list beginning with "mother" and ending with "Melody."

The girl watched him intently.

Danny reached for the slate. "What does 'muck-a-wiss' mean?" he wrote.

"It is his call. It means 'Come to me.' " Melody printed the words carefully.

"Me." Danny shaped the word, then said it several times until Melody joined in.

Later, when she was on her way home, she repeated the sound over and over. She was tremulous with happiness. She had learned to make a sound that had meaning. No longer would she have to reply to the frog or a cow in its way; she would have a word of her own to give back, a word that signified herself. Tomorrow she would ask Danny to teach her how to say his name. Happiness quickened her, and she started to run across the open fields.

The August days with their harvest moved into the golden quiet of September. The swallows had gone; neither among the rafters of the barn nor circling ecstatically in the air were they to be seen any longer. The songs of the singing birds were silenced; only small twitterings came from them now. Apples were falling from the trees in the orchard and Melody brought them into the kitchen in baskets, for Jennet was busy making apple butter. Jared was working with his sons in the fields so that potatoes might be dug and the rowen brought in before wind, rain, and frost took over the land.

No one spoke of the missing gray stallion. The township felt shamed that a horse had slipped through its net for the first time in all the years the Hue and Cry had existed; yet from no other quarter came word of the apprehension of either horse or thief.

Day after day Danny tried the remedies he knew to help Blue's swelling go down. He made the horse stand with his rear legs in the lake all one day, but it did no good; he moved rocks to form a mud wallow in which he made the horse stand for the day, but the leg only seemed to become more stiff, and its twitching muscles told of pain.

"Aye, but it's heat you're wanting and that's one thing I can't give you. Heat on the leg and a bed deep with straw and a manger of sweet hay." Danny leaned against the horse as he spoke, fingering his knife. Once he had killed a horse that had fallen on the race track and broken its forelegs. Death had been better than agony. But he had closed his eyes before he begged for forgiveness and sent the knife home. For a week he had not slept at night because of the dreams that haunted him.

A sharp sound reverberated on the air. Danny turned quickly and waved to the girl who had appeared out of the woods and was clapping her hands together.

Melody put down the bundles she was carrying and went to feel Blue's leg. She shook her head; then she stood in front of Danny and, closing her fists, rapped them hard on his chest.

"You must tell my father," she wrote quickly on her slate. There was a look on her face never there before. She knew what it was to suffer and not be able to speak.

"No." Danny shook his head.

Melody shaped a question mark with the fingers of her right hand.

Danny started to speak, then took the slate to write on it. "He'll give me away."

"Not against your will."

Danny put his head in his hands and rocked it back and forth.

Melody pointed to the sky. It was not blue as it had been for days past, but gray and hazy. "Storms soon," she wrote.

"Can you be sure about your father?" Danny wrote.

Melody seized the chalk and put both hands on her heart, nodding.

"Maybe," Danny said, "tomorrow."

Melody could not have said why she was so sure that Danny would be safe in her father's house; but she was. Jared would protect him as he had protected her. There were those who called Jared softhearted, but Melody knew that he had been the only one strong enough to build a bridge upon which she could cross to the world. He would do the same for Danny; how she could not say. She saw Danny's hands nervously fingering his knife. His eyes were straying from the horse to the lake and back again. No words needed to be written on the slate for Melody to dread the intent of those restless fingers. She pointed to the knife and held out her hands.

Danny shook his head furiously, then moved his hand in a quick gesture across his throat and made the same movement toward the horse. Blue was standing with drooping head, ears back and eyes half-closed. Even the hand moving suddenly before him did not startle him.

Melody stared.

Danny picked up the slate. "Life's not worth the living," he wrote. He handed the chalk to Melody.

She refused it. How to tell him all that had become hers–that life was not something to reject or set aside, that it was like the day when it came over the mountains: a space of time for doing. Her father had told her that one could not question the gifts one brought to the world, that one could only use them so that the world would be a kinder place because of one's presence in it. She had brought a strange gift with her, but her father had not doubted that it was meaningful, and she had accepted his faith. She shook her head. She could not write all that on a slate.

There would be a way, there would always be a way, Melody thought within herself.

Danny was picking up sticks and carrying them to the lair near the great rock where he slept at night. During the week, the nights had become cold, and he had given himself the comfort of a small fire in the dark when the smoke would not be seen. Melody gathered branches and added them to his pile. When there was enough wood for more than one night,

Danny signaled to her to stop, but Melody went on working. Twigs and branches interested her no longer. It was heavy boughs now that she was tugging at, closing her open hands around them, breaking them against her knee into burning lengths. Danny shrugged his shoulders. As well ask a beaver about his intentions.

A sudden sharp cry, more animal than human, pierced the air. Danny turned quickly and saw Melody holding her hand to her mouth.

"There now," he exclaimed aloud, "you've hurt yourself!"

He went to her and tried to take her hand in his to see the injury, but she shook it from him and looked at it herself. She puckered her lips in pain and ran from him to sit on a rock. He followed her and she held out her hand to him. A piece of wood had penetrated the flesh and was deeply embedded.

Danny looked at it closely. "Hold still now and I'll take it out for you," he said, bringing his knife from its sheath and holding the tip over her open palm.

Melody watched him as he dug for the sliver. His hands were grimy and the knife was broad, but, working cleverly with the tip, he started to edge the splinter from under the skin.

Suddenly Melody closed her palm around the knife and with her free hand pushed hard against Danny's shoulder. He toppled over into the water at the lake's edge, and she ran fast across the stones into the woods and toward the brook. She did not look back. She had what she wanted, and she knew that Danny would be no worse for a ducking. Of one thing she was now sure, that he would do no harm to himself or to Blue Lightning. The weary hours of the night might make his spirit sag with hopelessness, but, deprived of his only weapon, he was safe from self-harm. His legs were long and he might easily outrun her once he got on them again, but he did not know the way she took through the woods. Even to regain his knife, she doubted that he would risk being seen by others and come out into the open fields in broad daylight.

At the edge of the woods Melody paused and put the tip of the knife to the sliver in her palm. Her deft fingers removed it easily. She looked at the knife carefully, turning it in her hands. Its edge was sharp. Danny kept it so. She smiled. Her father would like that. He liked a man who kept his tools in working order. The skin of her palm was grazed where she had closed her hand on the knife, but no blood had been drawn. The handle fitted well to her palm. It was smooth with use. Initials had been carved into it: *D O'D*. The same as were on the saddle. She put it to her lips and kissed it. A flow of joy coursed through her being. She had something of Danny's with her; it was almost like having him. She put the knife into a pocket of her dress. She would guard the knife, as Danny was guarding Blue Lightning.

Walking slowly toward the house, she felt conscious of her strange treasure, but she did not feel that she was in possession of something to which she had no right. She had taken the knife for good reason; so Danny must have taken Blue Lightning for good reason. Her father would know, and he would know what to do. But would Rufus and Benoni agree with Jared in everything? Each of them were members of the Hue and Cry, and each member was pledged to do all in his power to return a missing horse found in his area to its rightful owner.

Melody felt the knife for reassurance. There would be a way, she told herself; there would always be a way.

Rufus and Benoni were hungry that night, and even Jared ate more than usual. The long day in the fields and the chill that had come on the wind toward sunset had sharpened their appetites and made them sparing of conversation. Jared was usually the one who brought news to the table, but he had not been journeying that week, and the only news he had was observations of the life around him such as any of them might make.

"I've not seen so many chipmunks all year," he said, "skipping along the stone walls, in and out of the chinks."

"They're readying themselves for the winter," Jennet replied, "as we all are. Twelve deep jars of apple butter I've stored already, and that will give us something to spread on our bread when the milk thins and lessens."

It was red squirrels that Benoni had been aware of, leaping from branch to branch in their sport, tossing jibes at him, as he worked below them.

"I'll go there tomorrow with my gun and get you enough for a dozen pies, Mother," Rufus said.

"Enough for one pie would be plenty," Jennet answered.

"No!" Benoni exclaimed. "Let them be. They do us no harm, and we've no need for other meat with the pig just slaughtered."

Rufus looked at his brother scornfully. "You're as tender-hearted as Melody."

Melody saw the look that passed between her brothers. She got up quickly to take Rufus's plate to the hearth and fill it again. In her haste to divert them, she forgot about the knife in her pocket. It slipped from her dress and landed on the hearth bricks with a dull thud. Melody put the plate down and reached to cover the knife with her hand.

Jennet exclaimed at the girl's clumsiness.

Rufus laughed. "That will just mean a little ash on my spoon to flavor the pudding."

"It wasn't your spoon that fell," Benoni murmured.

Only Jared saw what had happened. He got up from the table and laid his hand on Melody's, but she pressed hard against the hearth with the flat of her hand. The knife was longer than the reach of her hand. She could not cover it all. At one side the tip stuck out and at the other a portion of the hilt.

"Melody has something she is hiding," Jared said quietly; "don't frighten her."

Jennet let out a scream and came to stand by the hearth. Rufus and Benoni towered beside their father. Melody was shaking her head, her long hair swaying back and forth. Jared laid both hands tenderly on Melody's hand and looked at her as if there were only the two of them in the room. Melody yielded and let him take the knife, but she put her hands up to her eyes while he looked at it.

Jared turned the knife slowly. "It's a fine piece of English steel, not the like of what we'd see from one year to another in this land, and it's been kept sharp by one who knows how a tool should be treated." He reached behind him and laid it on the table.

Jennet looked at it fearfully. "What was she going to do with it–kill herself tonight?"

"Not Melody," Jared said, knowing his daughter well.

Rufus picked up the knife and examined it. "It's got initials on it." His fingers traced what his eye had told him. "*D O'D*, whatever that may mean."

Melody looked up at her father, then rose to her feet and put her hands on his shoulders to compel his attention. She pointed to her head and then to her eyes. She held her forefinger out and described a jagged line with it; then she put both hands tight over her heart.

"Melody says she knows where Blue Lightning is but she won't tell," Jared explained.

Rufus's shout might have lifted the roof. "Where is he?" he demanded of his sister. "Is he alive or dead? Oh, Mother, where's her slate? I've got to find out."

Jennet sat down heavily at the table. "You'll get nothing from Melody when she wants to keep it to herself."

Benoni remarked, as if he were thinking out loud, "Perhaps that's why the oats have been going down so in the bin this past week."

"Oats!" Rufus exclaimed. "If she's been feeding him, then he's alive; if he's alive and anywhere near, I'll find him; and if I find him, the reward will come to me!"

The others paid no attention to Rufus. Their eyes were on Melody. She was still standing on the hearth but she had bent down and was outlining a circle with a handful of ashes. She stepped inside the circle and motioned to her father, holding out her hand and drawing him into the circle with her. Father and daughter looked solemnly at each other; then Jared laid one hand on his heart and the other on hers as he gave her his word of honor.

He stepped out of the circle and faced his sons. "What Melody knows," he said quietly, "she will tell to only me."

Jennet sighed and nodded. It was the old story. Always it had been like that. "She trusts you, Jared."

"Then you'll tell us, won't you, Father; so we can bring the thief to justice and restore the horse to his owner?" Rufus demanded.

Jared shook his head. "I can't say, Rufus, until I know what Melody knows. Never yet have I been light with her confidence and I will not now."

"Even to see justice done?"

Jared paused for a brief moment. "Justice will be done, but there is more than one kind of justice," he answered his eldest son.

Benoni was the first to leave the room and go out of the house to the barn. Rufus followed him, walking heavily and wreaking some of his feelings on the door as he drew it shut behind him. Jennet commenced to clear the table and put the dishes in the iron kettle at one side of the hearth. Whatever conversation Jared and Melody had was not one that she would be apt to overhear.

Chapter Six

It was not until noon the next day, when Jared was in the field with his sons, that he told them what Melody had told him about Blue Lightning. They were sitting in the shade of an oak. There was little need for shade, as the sky was overcast and the wind had a raw edge, but the oak was a tree of noble girth and the three could sit at its base with their backs against its scraggy bark and still leave room between them. They unfolded their kerchiefs in which Jennet had placed thick slices of bread with slabs of cheese. They ate slowly and took turns drinking from the firkin of milk they had brought with them.

Neither of the boys had questioned Jared earlier about his talk with their sister. They knew their father well enough to know that he would speak in his own time and that no question of theirs could hasten that time. Rufus was impatient to know his story. Benoni sat quietly.

"I speak to you as men of honor," Jared began.

Rufus sat up straight and turned to face his father. Benoni went on drawing designs in the earth with a twig he held in his hand.

"Yes?" Rufus urged.

"Melody discovered by pure chance the hiding place of the horse and the rider. She has been going there day after day with food for each one."

"And to think I never noticed her!" Rufus exclaimed. "I might have followed her, and everything would be over by now."

Benoni said, "The oats did go down in the bin, but in a good cause, and that's better than when the mice get at them."

Jared went on with measured words, telling them Melody's story. When he spoke of the injury the horse had sustained which had resulted in a bad leg rapidly worsening, Rufus interrupted. "But we must get the beast to the barn and care for him!"

"That's what Melody wants."

"Let's go for him now, Father," Rufus said. "It's more important to get that horse in than to get these potatoes dug."

"I gave my word to Melody that nothing would be done unless we agreed to let the lad go free."

"And forfeit the reward?" Rufus was incredulous.

"Even so."

"And fail to bring a wrongdoer to justice?"

"Perhaps."

"Father!" Rufus said, amazement and scorn battling in his tone.

"He must be an uncommon thief," Benoni murmured.

"He's no horse thief at heart." Jared breathed more easily with half his story told. "As near as I can make out, he's an Irish immigrant who came to this land believing all he had heard about it—work, riches, quality; and since he has been here, everything has gone against him. He fled, not from justice but from hard luck, on a horse that was handy to him. Now the horse is injured and he can't travel. He's afraid and confused. He's desperate—"

"The knife!" Rufus exclaimed.

"Yes, Melody got hold of his only weapon and took it from him so that in his despair he would do no harm to himself or to the horse."

Rufus leaned back against the oak. "Why don't the dissatisfied folk stay in their own lands instead of coming here and cluttering up our country?"

"Freedom is the lure, Rufus."

"And money, I'll warrant."

"Yes," Jared agreed, "but I'll warrant you that with everyone who comes here there's a heart-urge that's more than the money. An adventure in good will is being worked out in this land of ours. We have profited by the blessings of freedom; let us not turn the tide away from others who would know those blessings."

Rufus had no reply.

"I'm sorry for the young people who come here thinking the way will be easy and then find that it is nothing but work and hard times and trials, as it is wherever one goes. But the strong of heart only grow stronger, and as they open their hands to labor and pour their sweat into the soil, they become as rightful a part of the nation as we who were born here. The lad Melody tells me of is young. He's had none to turn to that he could trust, and he thinks nobody cares what becomes of him."

"The sheriff will know what to do with him," Rufus muttered.

Jared shook his head. "In time, perhaps, when the lad sees what he should do."

"Father, do you mean you intend to shelter him here?"

"I do, Rufus." Jared spoke decisively. "Until the horse's leg is improved and the lad sees a better way to go than he has been going."

"But there's a heavy fine on those who are found sheltering a thief, and there's all forfeit of the reward!"

"I know that, Rufus."

Benoni lengthened himself out in the grass and put his arms across his face. As long as he could remember he had heard these altercations between his elder brother and his father–the hardness of Rufus coming up against the softness of Jared; yet invariably it was Jared who won. Benoni smiled to himself under the shield of his arms. He knew that Rufus would do what his father wanted him to do and that in the end it would prove to be the best way for them all.

They finished their luncheon in silence. Rufus felt certain that he could discover the thief's whereabouts. He would watch for Melody as she left the house, and he would follow her. The situation would then be in his own hands. He would return the horse to Captain Mallow in Portsmouth, give the boy over to the sheriff, and receive the reward. He would say nothing about his plan and much of it could be carried out under cover of darkness. When he returned with a hundred dollars in his pocket, his father would respect him for doing what any man would do–taking whatever opportunity offered to better himself in the world.

No more was said about the matter during the afternoon. Jared knew that it was useless to try to persuade Rufus to leniency, and furthermore there was half a field of potatoes to be dug. Rufus kept his face toward the house as he worked, but he never saw the flutter of Melody's dress anywhere except by the well or crossing the space to the barn. When they returned from the field, she was sitting on the doorstone carding wool as if she had nothing else to think about.

Rufus sat down beside her and offered her a flower he had found growing along the stone wall. It was one of the everlastings; its faded strawlike blossom would change little in color and not at all in texture through the months to come.

Melody took it happily and pressed it to her lips. She smiled at the brother who was so much bigger than she was. Rufus, in giving her such a flower, was giving her the symbol of everlasting love, and Melody cherished every token of affection. The sympathy of others did her little good, but evidences of love warmed some deep and lonely core within her. She tucked the flower into her dress. Even when Rufus went West someday, she would have this reminder of him.

Rufus watched her as she folded her hands in her lap, enjoying his presence beside her. She held a secret which he felt he would give a great deal to possess, but he loved her, and he knew that he could not do anything that would hurt her. If they talked together for a while, she might give him the information he was seeking. He did not want to wrest it from her or frighten her in any way. After he had done what he was determined to do, he could explain his reasons more fully, and she would understand.

On the stone beside her was her slate and chalk. Rufus picked up the slate and wrote on it. "What is the name of the lad who has Blue Lightning?" He placed the slate on her lap and handed her the chalk.

She shook her head. Turning to face her brother fully, she laid her hands on his knees; then she opened her mouth and put her tongue against her front teeth. A garbled meaningless sound came forth.

Rufus stared at her and she knew that she had failed in her attempt. She shook her head and smiled; then she tried again. This time she produced the sound she wanted. It was clumsy but unmistakable.

"Dan." She said it again as the look on her brother's face told her what his words could not. "Dan."

Rufus was as startled as if one of the horses had addressed him by name. Jared was approaching the doorstone.

"Father, she spoke to me!"

Jared said quietly, "I forgot to tell you, Rufus, that he's taught her to say a few words in this one week. That's more than I've been able to do in all the years of Melody's life."

"There's more to a man than horse thieving if he can do that," Rufus said soberly.

He turned toward his sister again and placed both hands on his heart. It was the sign they had used with her since she had been old enough to understand what respect of confidence was and that honor was something more than a word in a book. She stared at him with wide blue eyes full of belief and love; then her glad sound that was like the bleat of a lamb escaped her and she threw her arms around Rufus's neck. Rufus, holding her in his strong arms, rose to his feet, then lifted her so her head was higher than his.

Melody was happy. She knew now that she could trust Rufus and there was nothing to be feared. Benoni would take the side of his father, and Jennet would do what Jared wanted her to do, though she might make free with words of disapproval.

Rufus let his sister down to the ground gently and turned to his father. "I'll do whatever you and Melody want," he said. "There's something more in this than meets the eye or echoes on the ear."

"There is indeed," Jared replied. He placed his hand on his son's shoulder. "If the horse survives and we can persuade the lad to give himself to justice and all goes as it should, you shall have every penny of the reward." He laughed. "You're the only one in this household who would know what to do with such a sum!"

Rufus smiled and moved his head in agreement. But he knew all too well that it was too much like the rainbow's gold to count on that money.

"We'll seek them out first thing tomorrow morning," Jared said. "Melody will show us the way."

"Where are they hiding?"

"I know no more than you except that it is not far, less than a mile. Melody would not tell me the hiding place. I think she wants to be sure we will not turn him over to the sheriff until he has told us his story."

Melody preceded them into the house. Rufus followed her, calling to Jennet in his hearty way that he hoped the meal was ready soon, for he was a man with a hunger.

Jared paused for a moment on the doorstone. He did not like the look of the evening sky. Those tattered fragments of cloud in the west and the lusterless gleam of the setting sun spoke of rain before morning, and if the wind changed, the

80

rain would be cold. He was glad the potatoes were in, but he could have wished the Irish lad and his horse were in too, sharing the shelter of house and barn. Melody had reasons for what she did, and she must have one for her insistence that they go to find the two in the morning rather than at night.

Well, Jared thought to himself, the woods had shelter, and wherever the two might be, they would not fare ill, even in rain. By the next midday both would be safely housed, and Jared knew he could rely on the Austin family to aid the fugitives. He turned and went into the house, leaving the lowering sky and the keening wind for the cheer of his own hearth and the ample table Jennet had spread.

Chapter Seven

The September twilight soon faded into night, and a lamp was lit that filled the room with warmth and cheer. For the first time in many months, a log with long hours of burning in it was rolled onto the coals. During the evening and into the night, it would fortify the house against the dampness and chill of early autumn.

At the supper table, Melody guessed that their conversation was about Danny and Blue Lightning. She was not included in it, but she felt satisfaction at what she saw in their faces–the alert planning that marked Rufus's sharp eyes as he leaned across the table and talked with his father; the gentle acquiescence that was written on Benoni's face; and the deep concern in Jennet's as she looked from her husband to her elder son and entered into their scheme. Occasionally she threw a swift glance toward Melody and, seeing the girl's lips trembling with happiness, knew that all was well in her heart. She pointed to Melody's slate on the mantel and raised her eyebrows, but Melody shook her head. She needed no slow way of written words to follow the conversation. She had a way of her own.

Melody's gaze went back to the mantel. Beside the slate lay Danny's knife. That, more than anything else, could bring Danny to them. In his need of it he might even come seeking it, and that was what Melody prayed might happen. She wanted him to come proud and strong in spirit as a wayfaring man might come to the door, asking for shelter because he was weary and for food because he was hungry. She did not want them to search him out as they might an animal in its hole. She wanted him to come in a way worthy of him; to face her father eye to eye, to meet Rufus as an equal, to clasp hands with Benoni, and to turn to her mother as to one with a heart big enough to take him in. Perhaps Danny, tempted to recover his knife which was not only a weapon but a link with his past, might be drawn to their doorway tonight.

They were getting up from the table now and taking their dishes to the big kettle on the hearth. Melody knelt down by the kettle to tend to the washing. Jared sat on the oak settle with Jennet beside him, and the two boys went to the barn, swinging a lantern between them against the darkness.

In only a few minutes Rufus was back in the house again, bursting in with the wind behind him and a startled look on his face. "Mother! Father! Blue Lightning is in our barn!"

Jennet dropped the wooden bowl of beans she was shelling and stared at Rufus. Jared thought Rufus must have been seeing things. But when Benoni came rushing in with the same story, both Jared and Jennet followed their sons to the barn, leaving the door of the house wide open behind them.

Melody looked up from her work, surprised that they had all left the house. Running to the window, she saw the bobbling of the lantern in Benoni's hand and four figures disappearing into the barn. A new calf, she thought quickly, but none was due. She started to follow then changed her mind and went to close the door against the wind. She would not leave the house with Danny's knife on the mantel and no one there to welcome him. Returning to the hearth, she set herself to pick up the beans which Jennet had spilled in her excitement.

Ten minutes later they all returned to the house, just ahead of a squall of rain-laden wind that beat against the windows in sudden fury. Melody felt the vibration and saw rain streaming down the panes.

"The horse is all right until morning," Jared said, "and he's been cared for by one who has a hand for horses. It's not the lad's fault that he couldn't get the swelling down. I'm thinking that will take the skill of a horse doctor."

"Where do you suppose the poor lad is?" Jennet asked, going to a window and looking out into the rain-washed night.

"If he got the horse to shelter, he's sheltering some place himself," Jared answered. "Morning light will tell us much that we want to know."

Benoni was sitting on the hearth beside Melody, relating to her by means of her slate and a series of swift gestures what had taken place. Melody brought her hands together and a smile spread over her face.

Rufus added a smaller log to the fire to give a blaze, and Jared sat down again on the settle. Bed would call to them all soon, for it had been a work-filled day and no one could foresee what demands the morrow would make; but tonight there was wool to card, and Jared wanted to help Benoni with a chair design. The evening was still young, though it had gone into darkness.

Rain battered against the house and wind howled around the corners, but the family within were warm and busily occupied. Benoni brought his tracings to spread on the table for his father to see. Rufus helped his mother card wool. Melody sat on the hearth looking into the fire.

The rain softened in its gusts and the wind sighed as if it were growing tired, but the first wild night of many winter nights to come would not soon be tamed.

"The wind sounds like someone trying to get in," Jennet said dreamily, looking up at the window near her. Then she dropped her carding comb and a scream escaped her. "There is someone trying to get in!"

They all looked up quickly, hands arrested in what they were doing and eyes riveted on the window.

"There's nothing there," Rufus said.

Jennet nodded. "There was! A face. I saw a face. Jared, send one of the boys to the door."

Rufus started to go, but Jared called him back. "No, not you, Rufus. Let Melody go." He touched his daughter on the shoulder and pointed to the door.

Melody turned to him with the look of startled delight that sometimes marked her face. Jared signed that she was to open the door. Melody stood for a moment on the hearth, smoothing the folds of her dress; then she walked across the room and put her hand on the thumb latch.

She opened the door and looked out into the stormy night, but there was no one standing on the doorstone. She stepped out and held her hands high over her head, clapping them as loud as she could. Then, looking along the length of the house, she saw something like a shadow move in the darkness. She clapped her hands again and held them toward the shadow. Slowly it moved along the clapboards and came to stand near her. Melody took hold of Danny's hands and drew him onto the doorstone beside her, then into the house.

He was wet from the rain. His heavy black hair was plastered to his head and his face glistened in the lamplit glow of the room. Melody tried to draw him across the room toward the hearth, but he shook his head stubbornly and would not move from his stand near the door.

Jared crossed the room quickly. "I'm Jared Austin and I bid you welcome to our home."

Rufus followed him. "My name is Rufus. Welcome, stranger."

Benoni approached him. "I'm Benoni. Here's welcome to you."

Jennet flew across the room. "Why, he's nothing but a boy!" she exclaimed. She took his hands that hung limp and cold and held them in her warm ones.

Danny lifted his head and looked at her; then he dropped his head again and shook it from side to side. He was as bewildered by kindness as he had been embittered by hardship.

"Boys," Jennet said quickly, "take him to your room and put some dry clothes on him. He's wet through and cold, and he needs dry garments and warmth. I'll heat the pot again so there'll be something for him to put in his stomach. I'm thinking he hasn't had a good meal since he left his own home, and how long ago that was only he can tell us."

Rufus took Danny's hand and led him up the steep stairs to the room above where he and his brother slept. Benoni followed. Jared smiled to himself as he turned back toward the hearth. Jennet could always be trusted when her heart was appealed to, and the sorry-looking lad in his rain-soaked clothes and the half-starved look on his face had gone to Jennet's heart just as surely as a well-sent arrow into the bull's eye of a target.

Jennet quickly busied herself, assembling dishes and food. She moved the pot of stew back onto the fire to be heated for his supper. "He'll be needing a sip of perry to send warmth into his marrow," she said.

"I'll go downstairs for it," Jared offered, "and I'll bring up enough for us all. If the lad opens his mouth to do more than eat, he'll have some telling to do and we some listening."

Melody reached up to the mantel and took the knife down. She placed it on the table where her mother had laid a cup and a spoon and a fork for their guest; then she went to the settle and, tucking her legs under her, curled up in the corner near the blaze from the log. She felt quiet with happiness.

The boys and their charge came clattering down the steep stairs. Danny looked like a blend between them, with Rufus's trousers and a shirt of Benoni's, but their shoes had not been small enough for him, and so he walked across the floor barefoot. Jennet noticed how strong and clean his feet were and thought that he was one who had been taught to keep himself well. She motioned to the bench by the table and put a plate of food before him.

Jared thought how much taller the lad looked when he held his head up.

"Thank you, my lady. Thank you, sir," Danny said as he sat down at the table. He saw his knife lying on the polished wood. The first smile the Austins had seen on his face moved fleetingly across his features. He picked up the knife, felt its edge with his fingers, then slipped it into his belt. Having it again made him feel like a man. He glanced shyly at Melody on the settle, but her eyes were not on him. Without a word he picked up fork and spoon and ate the meal Jennet had placed before him.

Jared and Jennet and the two boys watched him in silence. When he had finished, Jennet took the plate away. "More you shall have tomorrow," she said firmly. "More tonight would be too much."

Jared was pouring out perry into small pewter cups which he handed to them all, the first to their guest, the last to Melody. Then they sat down at the table; Jennet beside the stranger, the boys opposite him, and Jared with his back to the hearth.

Danny looked around the table at them all, straight into the eyes of each one in turn. "I'm Danny O'Dare from County Donegal in the north part of Ireland," he said, aware that he owed them an introduction.

"It's a long way you've come from the place where you've been spending your life," Jared commented.

"Aye, a cruel long way it's been across the ocean to a strange land."

"He who travels has tales to tell," Jennet said softly.

"Is it tales you're wanting?" Danny looked around at them, half-smiling. "Arra, when I came to this land I thought I'd find gold on the streets, and all I found was a people working so hard they had no time for anything but sleep so that they could go on with their work the next day."

"There's no gold except for those who work," Rufus said.

"Tell us your story," Jared urged.

"Is it me you're after listening to?" Danny asked, looking around at them. He was surprised yet cheered by their interest.

They nodded.

"Safe be the storyteller," he murmured, as if he were asking a blessing. He glanced over his shoulder at Melody. She caught his glance and smiled at him, putting her two hands over her heart. Danny looked at Jared. "She's told me I can trust you."

"She told you the truth."

"Oh," Danny said, shaking his head, "I've learned there are not many in the world one can say that about, and I've not seen nineteen summers."

"How is it things have been so hard with you?" Jennet asked.

"The blessing of God be with you, my lady, but I think I was one born for sorrow, or so it seems. We were a family such as yours in a cottage in Donegal, near Kerrykeel in Knockallen where the sea rolls in your ears all day and the wind is fresh from the mountains in the heartland. Oh, it's a lovely land it is, for the green hills go down to the sea, and the air is so mild and moist that one season glides into the next, and you're no wiser for it except that the potatoes instead of being in blossom are in fruit. And the rain comes often and all the year."

"You worked your own land?" Jared asked.

"We worked the land, yes, but it was not our own, and there's no man in Ireland saving a rich man who can call the land his own. The best of our produce, the best of our stock, went to the estate manager every year and there was little enough we ever got for it, and the best that all Ireland raised was shipped across the sea to England. Were it not for the potatoes that flourished, I would have been hungry more often than full since I was a small child."

Jennet shook her head sorrowfully. "Poor lad," she murmured.

Danny smiled at her. " 'Tis no use being sad over one, for it was the lot of us all."

"You farmed the land but others took the profit?" Jared asked.

"It was my father who worked in the fields, and it was myself that helped him when my work in the stables was over. Always I had been a good hand with the horses, and they put me to work with them when I was a lad of nine, and it was the master himself who gave me my knife the first day I started work."

"It's a fine piece of steel," Jared commented.

Danny smiled, pleased that one of his two treasures was appreciated. "Soon I was not only caring for the horses but was helping to train them as well. Before I turned sixteen, I brought a little filly first to the finish line in one of the county races. For that the master gave me a saddle of my own. It's as fine a piece of leather as ever you'll see, but I wish he'd given my father more for his crops! There was little enough money ever to buy with, and little enough food we had for ourselves after the master and the estate manager and the agent all had their share. That was the year the crops failed and famine walked up and down the land. Aye, we could hear our hearts knocking against our ribs then, for there was not enough flesh to deaden the sound.

"But there was something else we heard too: the shipping merchants with their stories to tell of the land across the sea where there was gold for the getting. A man could eat his fill and a woman could carry her head high." Danny paused and looked around at his listeners.

They knew, as well as he did, that they were about to hear the part of the story for which they had been waiting. His heart was warmed by their interest, for he had within him the deep pleasure of telling tales. It was not so important to him that they believed what he had to say, though it was the truth he spoke.

He took a sip from his cup, then drew a deep breath and went on. "One day my Dada said to me, 'Danny boy, you're the oldest in the brood, and I've fifteen shillings saved against the day I die, but I want you to take it for passage to America.' Then another word he added: 'If all we hear is true, you'll be sending back more than fifteen shillings before you've been there a year.' Oh, but it was a heavy heart I had as I went about my tasks that day thinking that I soon would not be doing them again.

"Then the tale spread that there was a ship in at Belfast, soon to leave for Quebec. All a man needed to board the ship was his passage money and–that was fifteen shillings–and a bag of food for the sixty-day journey. My Dada filled a bag with potatoes and some dried herring and my Mam put in a loaf or two, but when their backs were turned, I returned most of the potatoes to the bin so there'd be room for my saddle.

"The night before I left they gave me the wake I'd never have in Ireland. From miles around the folk came, and the young lads and lasses were green as the fields with envy at my good fortune, and if anyone's heart was breaking it was not shown that night. There was tea in the big pot on the hearth and potatoes bursting their jackets in the coals. At dawn I had to leave, for the miles were long between me and Belfast, and the sack on my shoulder was heavy and the ship it sailed the next day.

" 'God guide you right,' said my father, but my mother's apron was over her face and I knew her heart was too burdened for words to come from her lips. 'Whist,' said I, 'but I'll be back before you've filled the cradle again, and my hands will be running with gold.' Then I turned and faced the road; east it was I would walk to Belfast, then west it would be by the light of my heart. A crowd of people was standing by the door of the cottage, waving and shouting, but I was not the one to look back for there was that in my eyes that was saltier than the seas that laved the coast of Donegal, and it was my heart that was heavy, not my sack."

"Poor lad," Jennet murmured, wondering how she would feel if she were seeing Rufus start off on the long road into another life.

"And was it a fine ship waiting for the tide at Belfast?" Benoni asked.

"Musha, it was a fine ship, with her ropes straining and her pulleys creaking and her sails spread to the breeze! The *Darling of the Waves* was her name and a good master was in charge of her. She was not the only one. There were other vessels ready to cast loose when wind and tide gave the word. And the people! 'Sure and all Ireland is here!' I said to myself, for it was not just the ones crowding the decks I saw, but the spectators lining the shore and the rowboats with gay banners streaming from them that dotted the water. Everyone was singing or shouting! Men were waving their hats and women their kerchiefs, and there was not a long face to be seen until the cannon boomed from the shore and the anchor chains grated.

"Oh, then there were tears falling into the water and prayers flung aloft, and many a heart longing to turn the tide as the world of one's birth slowly passed from view." Danny paused as if he had not the heart to say what he had felt during that hour when the ship took hold of wind and tide and faced into the unknown, while all that was known and dear grew misty on the horizon.

Benoni leaned across the table. "I've not seen the sea except in pictures, but it must be a fine world of water."

"Aye, a fine world it is indeed," Danny said, "and the first forty days were the best. There were small places below deck for us to sleep and keep our provisions, but most of the time we spent on deck. Sure and it was like a town with the people following the life of their choice! A schoolmaster was there who gathered the children around him and gave them lessons. Whoever had a trade and the tools with him plied it. Had I a shilling to my name I might have had a pair of shoes made by a master cobbler.

"There were chickens and pigs in boxes and pens, and a cow who stood the journey well, but the milk she gave was given to the children. Stoves were provided on deck and whatever was cooked was flavored well with salt from the sea. Women did their washing, as women will, and on bright days such an array of garments fluttered below the rigging as made the *Darling* look as if she were on parade. The captain knew the winds as a cleric his letters, and by dint of skillful tacking we sped like a bird. Talk filled the air from morn till night. Everyone on the ship was in search of freedom and fairness, as well as work and riches. They were all smarting under the injustice they had suffered too long, and they wanted a better life for their children. They knew that in the homeland there were far too many people for too little land, far too many workers wanting too few jobs, and in the new land it was said there was room and work for all.

"Eating as light as I could, there was no food left in my sack at the end of forty days. Only my saddle. I put my head on it to sleep and still it had the good smell of the horse to it, but that couldn't feed a man. Closing my eyes, I saw the green of meadow and hedge and potato patch, but that couldn't feed a man.

"The ship supplied passengers with drinking water and sometimes there was broth to be had from one of the cauldrons of victuals boiling on deck, and people were kind. If a man gave me a piece of fried meat, I could make it last the day, and once a woman gave me a baked pie that fed me for three days! There was not a man or woman on that ship who could not remember what it was like to be hungry either in the famine summer of '22 or the cold winter of '29. The memory made them kindly disposed to anyone who was hungering; but glad we all were when we reached the banks of Newfoundland and put out lines to catch fresh cod. Not a few here and there, but dozens, hundreds! Enough for everyone to eat his fill for once."

"Was it fair weather all the way?" Rufus asked.

"Oh, it was not! There were days when the howling of the wind through the rigging and the moaning of the sea were enough to tear the heart from one. Only the shouts of the officers telling the sailors what to do let you know that someone else had a will as well as the storm."

Jennet shuddered and put her hands to her eyes.

"Sixty-two days out of Belfast the breeze freshened and we knew we were nearing land. There was none yet in sight, but the west wind coming clean from forest and meadow thinned the heavy saltiness of the ocean air. In spite of the weariness of the limbs from the cramped quarters, it was good to be alive then! The *Darling of the Waves* raced over the ripples like a horse over the miles when he gets the wind of home in his nostrils. And a good wind it was, sweet with the fragrance of hay, sweet with the breath of the forest.

"That night the beam of a lighthouse reached its fingers across the water, and sails were furled to hold our speed. The master of the ship came among us as we crowded the rails. 'Tomorrow we land on the neap tide,' he said. 'Tonight you shall eat from the ship's stores.' So we feasted well that night on biscuits and slush and fresh cod from the sea, and those who could make music made it for the rest of us. Where we would all be the next night none of us knew, and whether we would see each other again none knew, but we little cared, for the gates of the New World were opening to us and there wasn't a person there for whom the future wasn't as bright as the lighthouse gleam on the water. Sure, I thought of my mother that night, as I dropped to my knees to pray, for she it was who taught me to pray."

Danny's voice had been growing softer as he came near the end of his tale. Jennet gazed at him searchingly. He looked like a weary child, and she longed to put her arms around him and soothe him into slumber as she would one of her own.

"And you landed the next day?"

"We did, and in luck I was. There was a wagoner on the quay with a load of lumber he was taking down to the States.

He wanted help with the load and a man handy with horses; so I hired myself out to him and little I cared what I did so long as there was a place for my saddle in the wagon and some food to put under my belt. That was all I needed."

"It's sleep you need now," Jennet said, putting out her hand and laying it on Danny's.

He nodded.

"Come, then."

He got up from the table, looking almost as dazed as a walker in a dream. "Is it a bed you're putting me in?" he asked, the incredible making his voice fall to a whisper.

Jennet nodded and beckoned to Rufus and Benoni. "The boys will show you where and make you comfortable with them. See you put an extra cover over him," she cautioned Rufus.

Jared spoke suddenly. "Danny?"

"Sir?"

"I'll be glad if you don't show yourself tomorrow."

Danny looked puzzled; then understanding broke over his face. He smiled in assent and the three boys left the room, going up the stairs to the bedroom.

"You'll hide him then for a while?" Jennet asked in a whisper.

"It will be easier to hide the boy than the horse."

Jennet clapped her hands to her mouth. "The horse!" she exclaimed. "He's told us nothing about the horse."

"That will be for another evening," Jared said as he walked toward the settle.

Melody was fast asleep, curled round like a kitten with her head on her hands and her brown hair fallen over her face. Jared slipped his arms underneath her and picked her up, carrying her up the stairs to her bed under the eaves as easily as he would a bundle of wool from a sheep's back.

When he returned to the room, Jennet had banked the log with ashes and was opening their bed which stood against the wall.

"What music there is in the lad," she said. "I could listen to his talking for more hours than a clock can say."

"There's an old saying that we find at the end of every journey what we took with us," Jared replied. "Danny has come a long way, but at the end he may have found something that's a match to the music within him."

Jennet climbed into bed and drew the coverlet over her. "Put out the lamp, Jared," she said, but she was almost too far over the border of sleep to see him as he did it. He waited a few minutes, then lit a stub of candle which gave a lesser light.

Jared stood by the fire, thinking; soon he went to the cupboard near Jennet's loom where her wools and dye pots were kept. He could not tell what colors were in the pots, for the light of the candle gave little revelation, but leaning over, he lifted the covers one by one and smelled the contents. This was green, for the telltale odor of indigo was lessened by mixing it with flowers of goldenrod and alum; green would not do for his purpose. He replaced the cover and leaned over another pot. The smell of sassafras caught his nostrils. The yellow and orange color it gave would not do either; so he covered it again. Here was pokeberry, but the crimson it yielded would not serve him.

The two remaining jars he brought over to the hearth. Here was black: sorrel boiled for hours with logwood and copperas; and here was indigo blue. He stirred the blue gently and the vile odor that tingled his nostrils made him smile at what he knew proclaimed the strength of the dye. Bark of butternut and flowers of sumac and goldenrod had gone into this. He mixed the contents of the two pots. Rank and powerful, this would withstand the elements that might lessen other dyes—body heat, dew, or rain; and no gently licking tongue would be able to endure the taste.

Jared put a taper in the fire to light the lantern; then he snuffed out the candle. Lantern in one hand, dye pot in the other, he went to the barn and into Blue Lightning's stall. Talking easily all the while, he ran his hand over the horse as his eyes became accustomed to the light in which he would have to do his work. Blue nickered softly, almost secretly, and the two talked together in the dim light shed by the lantern while the rain pattered steadily on the roof, and the other animals sighed in sleep or munched an almost forgotten cud.

An hour later when Jared returned to the house, there was in the barn no gray horse with silver streaked mane and tail; but there was a horse midnight black from forelock to fetlock, with a black mane clipped short like a work horse and a tail that fell to the hock and not to the hoof.

The dye pot was empty and the candle in the lantern had burned out, but Jared had not traveled the space between barn and house for near twenty years without being able to travel it in darkness.

Chapter Eight

Jennet was the first one up the next morning and she was soon ready for the day. She removed the ash from the log and blew fresh life into the fire. She swung a large kettle over the blaze and into it went pottage enough for her family with an extra handful of meal for the lad sheltering under their roof. Jennet stirred it as it thickened; then she swung it away from the blaze so that it might go on simmering slowly.

She thought of Danny as she went about her early morning tasks, for her heart had been touched as much by the hungry look in his face as by the moving tale he had told. She knew she would not be content until the thin look went from him and his body filled out as a grown boy's should.

Jennet glanced around the kitchen. Everything was in readiness for the morning. Only the floor remained to be swept, but that was Melody's task and Jennet knew the girl would attend to it as soon as she came downstairs. Jennet took her cloak down from the peg on the wall where it hung. Throwing it over her shoulders, she ran to the barn to see how the fine gray horse that had caused such excitement looked in the morning light.

Jared was standing by the hearth with Melody beside him, her slate in his hands, when Jennet came running back to the house. Her hair had been tossed by the morning wind and consternation was in her face.

"Such talk you men have been making about a noble gray stallion," she exclaimed indignantly, "and all I see in the barn this morning is a broken down beast as black as a starless night! I'd not give a penny for him, nor hazard my life for him, either."

"Look in your dye pot, Jennet."

Jennet stared at Jared; then she opened her cupboard door. Two dye pots stood uncovered and empty. A thin film that had hardened against their sides proclaimed the colors they had once held.

"I'll thank you for mixing more dye today in case there's a spot needs retouching," Jared said.

Jennet nodded. "They'll be full by nightfall. Oh, Jared, I might have known your artistry did not stop with walls!"

Sitting around the table at the morning meal, the Austin family discussed in low tones something of what was to be done. Danny was to remain in the upper bedroom all the daylight hours and not come down to the kitchen until darkness gave them safety. Jared had work to do in another township and was soon leaving with his paints and brushes, but he would be home by evening. Rufus and Benoni would finish the harvesting. Jennet and Melody would go about their household tasks.

"Must the lad stay hidden all day?" Jennet asked.

"Yes, and for many days perhaps," Jared replied sternly. "It would do no good for him to be seen. We cannot claim him as kin, and anyone hearing that rolling voice of his would know there was something behind it."

Jennet agreed. There were times when she did not question Jared's decisions and this was one of them. "I'll do what I can to take down the swelling on the leg."

"I'll work on him when I get home," Jared said, "but your hands are sure and your head has a store of knowledge."

"If it's not in my head," Jennet said with a laugh, "it may be in my herbal."

After they had gone, each one to his task, Jennet took Danny a basin of water for washing and the treasured volume of Mr. Whittier's poems to help him pass the hours. Danny smiled broadly when he handed her the empty bowl in which Rufus had brought him a generous share of the morning's pottage.

"Sure and there's strength for a man's heart in that," he said.

"And for his body too," Jennet answered.

When she returned to the kitchen, she took her treasured herbal from the fireplace cupboard and consulted it for the best method of reducing a swelling. Page after page she read, seeking a remedy for swelling of joints in man or animal, but she found neither potion nor liniment in which she felt she could put her trust. There was one remedy she knew of, and it was written in no book; yet she had used it with success.

Two winters ago when Jared had fallen to the prevailing distemper–typhus they called it–she had administered decoctions of the plant internally and applications externally. In a short time the fever had abated. Jared had been on his feet and back at work sooner than others in the township who had sickened. She had none of the ingredients at hand; yet they were easily obtainable, for it was the time of year when the plant grew abundantly along the roadsides.

Jennet went to the door and clapped her hands above her head. She kept clapping them until Melody appeared, her arms full of onions whose pliant stalks she had been platting together to hang for winter use. When she saw that her mother wanted her, she put down the onions and came running to stand beside the doorstone.

Jennet handed Melody an empty basket. On the girl's slate she roughly drew a picture of a tall flower drooping with a weight of blossoms.

"Joe Pye's weed?" Melody wrote.

Jennet nodded and signed that the basket was to be full. Melody took it over her arm and went off down the road.

Jennet watched her go. Odd that the girl should remember the name of the Indian who had shown the settlers how to use the weed to cure fever. It had been called feverwort or sweating plant for so many years now that Jennet never thought of it as anything else. But Jared's way of introducing the girl to knowledge had always been by way of telling stories. No doubt he had made the Indian more real to her than the properties of the plant.

When Melody returned with her basket full of the soft-textured, pale purple flower heads, Jennet put them in a cauldron of boiling water and brewed them over the fire, stirring frequently and sipping now and then until she was sure of the strength. Melody helped her mother carry the cauldron to the barn while Danny watched from his window, glad that Blue was to have the heat applications which would soon take down the swelling.

Jennet cared for the horse all day, changing hot cloths as soon as they cooled and inducing some of the decoction into the horse by mixing it with a little bran. When Jared returned at dusk, he joined Jennet in the barn and helped her. Anyone passing along the road and seeing the light of the lantern shining through chinks in the barn might have thought it was a new calf Jared Austin was helping into the world or a foal who found entrance hard, for a lantern seen after dark in a barn meant little else.

"Too much heat may make the skin sore," Jared said at last. "We'd best leave the horse until morning."

Jennet felt the leg when she took the cloths off. "If it's gone down at all, it's only by the least bit."

"It took more than a day to put it in that condition," Jared reminded her. "It will take more than a day for the swelling to go down."

They left the barn and went to the house. Danny had joined Rufus and Benoni at the table and Melody was ladling out a meal of potluck for them all, but none would touch it until Jared asked the blessing. They ate with relish and with more dispatch than usual for each one knew there was something ahead which could not come till the meal was done and the table cleared of its dishes. When that time came, they turned to Danny almost as if there had not been a night and a day between his last words.

"Tell us how you put Blue Lightning's back under your saddle," Jared said.

Danny laughed softly. "It's a storyteller you're making of me with wanting a tale two nights running!"

Melody got up from the table and sat down on the floor near her father, leaning against his legs and putting her head in his lap. He could see her lips moving as if she were trying to form a word and thought that perhaps Danny had been teaching her that day. Jared smiled to himself, wondering if he who had never been a real trader when it came to horse-flesh had made a good bargain at last.

"Safe be the storyteller then," Danny exclaimed as he began the tale whose end they all knew, for it had been in their own kitchen.

"A long weary way it was, that journey from the Provinces down to the States," Danny said, "but I was like a man following a rainbow for the pot of gold at its foot. Little I cared for the journey. Through a wild land it was, passing more trees in an hour than I had seen in my lifetime. What towns we passed were small—a store, a tavern, a blacksmith, and always a Meeting House built plain like a barn but worthy for worship. Money was scarce and people seemed to pay in kind, but that was something I had none of, and money was what I needed.

"I lost count of the days, there were so many; and tired my legs were from trudging by the horses, keeping them on the road while the man who had hired me sat back on his load and took his life easy. But my saddle was in the wagon and a burden it would have been on my back.

" 'Sure and the spring of the year is a lovely time,' I said to myself as we came into an open countryside where fields were set off by stone walls and the land looked cared for. We passed copses of honeysuckle and wild roses with the air sweet enough for a man to drown himself in and the birds flitting about like angels. I liked the look of the people I saw, for they seemed in possession of the good things of life. I liked the look of the cattle in the fields and the young lambs, just like the ones in Ireland, and I thought, 'When the logs are delivered, I'll get work on this land, for it's a good land; it is indeed.' "

"New Hampshire land, I'll warrant," Benoni whispered to his father.

"It was at a town by the sea that we delivered our logs to a shipbuilder. Glad I was at the sight of ships in the making! In time, I thought, they'll be crossing the ocean, bringing people from the old land where hope is dust under their feet to this new land where hope soars like the wings of a bird. 'Tomorrow morning I'll pay you five dollars for the journey,' the teamster said to me that night.

"We went out of the town a short way to pasture the horses. I took the sack with my saddle in it and made myself a bed under a blossoming tree, and I prayed that night, so thankful I was and so sure of my powers of earning that I knew it would not be long before there would be money on its way back to Ireland. The teamster went to a tavern in the town, and we agreed to meet on the morrow. That was the last I saw of him."

"The last you saw of him?" Jared queried as if he had not heard Danny aright.

The lad nodded and what gaiety there had been in his face gave way to smouldering anger.

"Aye, I was up at the sparrow's chirp, wiping the dew from my face and shaking it out of my hair, but there was neither wagon nor horses where both had been the night before, only their tracks in the dust of the road. I went to the nearest tavern, but the man winked at me and said he could not tell one teamster from another and how would he know where mine had gone? I went to tavern after tavern, but it was the same story and the men laughed at me, as if it had been a rare joke that I had been fooled. They told me I'd have to sharpen my wits to make good in America.

"I had no money, and hungry I was as a young wolf cub. I saw people passing down the street and asked where they were going. 'To work in the mill,' a man said. I followed the people and I got work along with them. Thirteen hours a day it was and at the end of it I had fifty cents in my pocket. I thought it was the wealth of the land, but there was not much left after I'd had a meal or two and got new soles for my boots."

"Where did you live?" Jennet asked.

"Under the tree where I first slept. I kept my saddle hidden in a stone wall, but I brought it out every night to pillow my head. I came to hate the mill–the noise and the din, and my hands felt clumsy; but at least the work meant money in my pocket, and money meant food and a new pair of breeches when mine wore through at the seams.

"By midsummer there were some horses turned out to pasture in the field where I slept. I was happy then, for when I lay under the tree at night I could hear the thudding of hoofs on the grass and the snorting of nostrils. Sometimes they'd come near me and I'd feel their breath on me, warm it was and the smell of grass was in it. One horse in particular became my friend. He was the dappled gray stallion. He came near me at night and I brought him things to eat, a carrot or an apple.

"One dark night I jumped on his back, and we rode around the field together with only the wind to share our joy and a star or two to see us. 'Sure and it's a free land,' I said to myself, 'and if the teamster made free with me for a month of days, why shouldn't I make free with this horse?' Perhaps it was wrong, but I'd long since ceased praying to God, and my mind was dulled from the clacking of the reels, and I was tired of being a laughingstock because my speech and my manners were different. So I took what money I'd saved and kept buried, and I knew that I had enough to buy me a bridle.

"The next night when the gray came trotting up to me, so friendly and gentle, I slipped the bridle over his head and put my saddle on his back. The two of us cantered around the field and over the stone wall, and I cared not where we went so long as it was inland and away."

"When did you do that?" Jared asked.

Danny thought for a moment. "It was a night the moon set early and now the moon has filled her horn and is on the wane. Four nights we rode and three days we spent in hiding. I fed myself from apple trees and blackberry bushes and watered myself as the horse did. 'Tomorrow I'll seek for work,' I said to myself one night, 'for I've put enough space between me and the sea so that no one will know I've a horse not my own.' The next day I stopped in the first town I came to and went into the store, but the first thing I saw was a handbill describing my horse and offering a hundred dollars reward for the gray's return! That was the first time I realized what I had done. I knew then that I was a hunted man and that all I could do was escape."

"But how did you escape?"

"Oh, I've not ridden horses to the winning post in the County Donegal races for nothing! And the gray had been bred for speed! We left that town like a swallow on the wing. I was miles away and hiding in the woods an hour later when an army of men hot in pursuit went down the road after me. For a week I dodged and hid, and I kept my knife sharp for I'd vowed I'd kill myself and the gray before I'd give ourselves up.

"Then the gray lamed himself and I knew I'd have to find a hiding place where he could have rest. I passed this house one night, feeling safe for once, as there was music and merrymaking going on in the barn, and the horses tied outside gave me to know that I'd leave no telltale tracks if I found shelter somewhere near. Soon I passed a road so overgrown that I knew it was no longer used, but I thought it must lead somewhere. It did–to a small lake. The moon was shining on the water and I thought to rest ourselves there a bit. When the gray's leg improved, the countryside might then have lost hope of finding us. In a few days or a week, I thought I'd go on my way again.

"The world was against me, of that I was certain, and I felt sore at heart. There was no hope now in God or man and I knew I'd done things that would make even my own mother disown me. I was full of hatred and bitterness, and my hands held in them little power for good."

"Then Melody found you?" Jennet asked.

Danny shook his head. "I found her. I'd been exercising the gray up and down a piece of the overgrown road, and when I returned to the lake she was there, sleeping in the sun. I might have killed her with my knife, but I didn't think she was real."

Jennet put her head in her hands as she thought of how she had watched Melody disappear into the woods that Sunday afternoon.

"Why did you come down to us that stormy night?" Jared asked.

"To get my knife back. A man is helpless without a knife."

"You weren't afraid of us?"

"No. She told me I could trust you." Danny looked at Jared beseechingly. "You won't give me up to the law, will you now?"

"Not against your will."

"My will?" Danny faltered, wondering if he had any such possession after the events of the past few months.

Rufus leaned forward. "I've no mind to turn the lad over to justice, Father, but what are we to do? We Austin men are all members of the Hue and Cry. You know the pledge as well as I do. How can we be true to our trust and not turn Danny over to the sheriff and see that the horse goes back to his owner?"

"The Hue and Cry," Danny asked, "what is that?"

"An organization that has branches in every community to help support the law by apprehending horse thieves. We have pledged ourselves to see justice done. Here in America every citizen shares in the order and peace of the land."

"No one helped me when the teamster robbed me of my wage," Danny countered bitterly.

Jared reached his hand across the table and placed it on Danny's. "I'm sorry for that, but amends will not be won by retaliation. Tell me, Danny O'Dare, do you understand about handicaps?"

"Arra, I do. I'd not have run horses in races without knowing about such things."

"The man who did you wrong is one of the handicaps this nation has to run with."

Silence fell over the group around the table. Jennet was the first to break it. "Jared has always been one to put his faith in the goodness of God, Danny," she explained consolingly, "and he's not been my husband these many years without my feeling that way too."

"Sure and I once had a great faith," Danny replied, "but it's been driven out of me by the troubles I've had since I left my old home–by the ship and the journey and the mill. Sometimes I feel choked with the hatred that rises in me against the cruelness of men."

Melody had risen to her feet and was leaning against her father, looking across the table at Danny, wondering what all the long words were he had been saying and wishing they were written in a book so that she could read them. Danny responded to her glance. She smiled at him with a wide arc of understanding that made him smile too.

"I thought I had lost all my faith," he said quietly. "But it seems there's a small grain left. And it's your girl that God has used to nourish it."

Chapter Nine

The days slipped into a week and the changes wrought were more marked in Danny than in Blue Lightning. Jennet's care, the interest of Rufus and Benoni, Melody's wide-eyed wonder, and Jared's quiet steadiness all contributed to make Danny feel like a person again. His body had begun to fill out, and his face was losing its gaunt, strained look. One day when Jennet brought him his noon meal, she was startled to realize what a handsome lad he was with his dark hair smooth and heavy on his head, his keen eyes, and the color mounting into his cheeks. He had a rangy build that would never carry much weight and small neat hands and feet.

Danny kept to the upper bedroom during the day, reading in the morning and doing tasks for Jennet. Melody spent much time with him and sometimes he read to her from her favorite book, the Bible. He talked to her too. Jennet, hearing his low voice, marveled at the patience in so young a person as he worked through the hours of an afternoon to teach Melody a single word. But the joy on the girl's face and the satisfaction on the boy's were worth all the time spent when, that night around the supper table, Melody would open her mouth and say the word. The sound was harsh and grating and there was no music in it, but the meaning was unmistakable.

There was little change with the horse. During that week Blue Lightning stood in his stall with his bad leg poised so that it rested on the tip of the hoof with no weight bearing on it. The most tempting mash and the sweetest hay did little to coax his appetite. His head drooped and his eyes were listless. But Jennet continued her applications and each one of the others rendered some particular care. On the eighth day a change for the better took place. The swelling began to go down, though the stiffness remained. Jared renewed the dye on coat and mane. In the evening after darkness fell, Rufus and Benoni took turns walking the horse slowly around the barnyard to try to stimulate action.

"You can't hide the two forever," Rufus protested later that evening to his father as they stood in the barn rubbing Blue's leg.

"It's been little more than a week," Jared reminded his son.

"But the countryside is still alert to the disappearance of the horse," Rufus said. "I heard talk today, when I took those sacks of potatoes to the store, that Colonel Benton was going to enlist the militia to search every farm in the county. There's more than one who can testify to the stallion's having been seen in this township, and the search will be a thorough one."

Jared shook his head. "The lad is stronger than when he came, and the horse is improving slowly. Changes on the outside must indicate changes within."

Benoni looked up from the leg he was rubbing. "Why don't you want to turn him over to the sheriff, Father, when that is what will happen to him sooner or later? Is it because of Melody?"

"Perhaps, but not entirely. Danny has come to a free land. I'd like to have him understand that freedom is every man's choice between doing right and wrong, but that the man who succeeds is the one who puts his choice on the side of right."

That night, after the others had gone to their beds, Jared sat by the fire talking with Danny. At supper Melody had said her father's name for the first time in her life. Harsh and formless and shaped into a single syllable, as it had been by her, it proclaimed an identity. At the sound of it, something within Jared had turned over with joy.

"How is it you have such patience with the girl?" Jared asked Danny.

"Sure and I've not worked with dumb animals for years back without having a bit of patience," he replied. "It's not what you say with them as how you say it."

Jared moved his head in agreement.

"But Melody has got what no animal has," Danny said quickly, "and that's the ability to speak. Are there no schools in this land where they teach the deaf? There are such in the old country."

Jared nodded slowly. "There is a school, though it's not free."

"Is there no money to send the girl to it?"

"No."

"Is there no one who cares?"

"In some townships they might raise the money, but I doubt if that would be so here, and it would take a deal of persuading for the girl's mother to accept people's bounty when she's had so much of their contempt."

"Tell me about Melody," Danny said, "and safe be your storytelling."

Easily, as he might to one with whom there was perfect understanding, Jared told Danny about Melody from the time she was born and how he had unconsciously given her the name that was to stay with her. A peaceful, happy babe she had seemed, but when she was a year old they had been forced to realize that she was different from other children.

" 'Tis strange, at times, the blessing of God," Danny murmured.

Jared looked at him quickly. "It's been hard for her mother, what with the way some of the townsfolk felt, but I thought it was something to use as best we could. From the start we sought to train the child to rely on herself. It was her mother who taught her to do things as she placed her hand on shoestring or button, spoon or ladle, and slowly the girl learned the ways of a woman about a house."

"And you?"

"I'd put her hand on a pencil and guide it till she made the letters that would grow into words. One day I was doing some hammering and it was thus we learned that she received vibrations. From then on, what with handclapping and such, we taught her to use vibrations. Melody and I would lie on the grass on a summer day, ears pressed to the earth, and in time she could tell the difference between cows tramping down the lane and a horse trit-trotting over the road. She learned to place her ear to the ground and get as much meaning from the vibrations passing through it as she could from those in the air."

"Praise God!" Danny exclaimed.

"She's grown well, and since she was a small thing her own curiosity has served her," Jared continued. "She's lived in our hearts and that's the best place for a child, but soon she'll reach a parting of the ways, and there'll be need for a decision about her life."

"Even without words she seems to understand everything."

"No," Jared said firmly, "not everything. She understands the good in life and in people. It's not been possible for me yet to find the way to explain the evil."

"Heaven keep her from such knowledge!"

"She expects those she knows to do right. I'd be at a loss what to tell her if they ever did wrong."

"Does she know many people?"

"Hardly more than the household and the near neighbors. And now you."

Danny smiled. A month ago he had not known Melody existed; now he was surprised to find how much her presence made his world. "Please God she'll always think well of me!" he exclaimed.

"Please God and she will."

Danny looked sharply at Jared. "Sure and you sound like my own father," he said, "for your words are kin to those that lay often on his lips. 'Please God,' he used to say, 'and let the world do what it likes with you.' "

Jared moved the log on the hearth and covered it with ash against the morning. "I've work to do out of the township, Danny. I'll not be back here to sleep for three nights after this night."

"The weather is turning to cold, if the signs in the sky are the same the world over."

"Yes, that sunset meant change. It may freeze tonight. It may rain tomorrow, but that's winter when my work as a journeyman painter is roused and that of a farmer slumbers."

Danny put his hand earnestly on Jared's shoulder. "They'll not give me away when you're gone?"

Jared shook his head. "You have the word of everyone in this household. Honor means much to us. We give it to others and expect it from them in turn."

They said good night and good-by, shaking hands like men. Danny went up the stairs to the bedroom and Jared crossed the room to his own bed where Jennet was waiting for him. She was still awake, though she had lain as quietly as one who sleeps.

"Jared," she whispered, "how long will you go on hiding the lad?"

"I've done what I can with him, Jennet. Now I think it will be up to Melody to do the rest. They are the same age. They hold much in common. He will soon have to explain his position to her; and if it is without honor, he will find it hard to tell her what she cannot understand."

"I'm fond of the boy, Jared. I'll shield him till you get back."

"I know you will, Jennet, and I'm of a mind that soon he'll need no more shielding. He's got something in him that's rising fast. He'll do the right thing."

Jared had soon got into bed and was pulling the blanket over himself, for the room was cold. "I'm riding off on Midnight tomorrow," he said.

"Not Pepper?" The announcement that Jared would not take his own horse surprised Jennet.

"No. I want to leave one fast horse in the barn. The boys might need him. Danny might need him."

"Danny!"

"Yes. If the men come searching our barn for Blue Lightning and the lad wants to escape, you must let him."

"Jared!" Jennet was wide awake now.

"Yes, and if he rides off on Pepper, you are to give him a paper that I have placed in the Bible."

"The paper has his name on it?"

"It has, but he will not see it unless he uses it as it should be used."

Jennet smiled into the darkness of the room. "You have written it with sympathetic ink?"

"I have. It is safer that way."

"Yes, it is safer."

"If a time comes when Danny should have the paper, will you tell him what it is and how to read it?"

"I will, Jared."

Now it was Jared's turn to smile into the darkness of the room. "On the paper I wrote that Pepper is my gift to him. Danny can ride where he likes and find work to do, and he'll ride like a man, for the horse will be his in his own right."

Should that happen, Jennet thought, she would keep a packet of food in readiness–some journey-cake and some cheese, enough to last the boy for a day or two. "I'll be ready, Jared, for whatever may come," she said. Her voice sounded small and compliant in the silence of the sleeping house.

In the room above, Danny leaned on his elbows across the sill of the window. Rufus and Benoni were sound asleep in the bed the three of them shared. Their breathing came evenly. Outside a few flakes of snow were borne on the wind. The snow, or the quietness, or perhaps the house itself, made Danny see himself for what he was–a poor immigrant lad from Ireland with the past washed away forever and no future before him but what he could fashion. What future could he make, he asked himself, while he was branded as a horse thief? Yet no one in the Austin household had said that to him; only his own soul.

No, in the house they had treated him as one of themselves. He might have been another son for all the way they acted. Surely Melody knew he was a thief. But how could he explain what he had done and why; how could he, if she had no knowledge of the evil ways men take when they are driven by fear and desperation? His heart felt heavy within him, for he knew he must speak before many more days had passed. There was something in him now that made him want to share with her the full tide of his life.

"Dear God in heaven," Danny murmured, dropping to his knees and covering his face with his hands. Prayer rose within him like a spring newly opened. It was a recourse he had left behind him when he thought the world had turned against him and one wrong deed had led to another.

When he got into bed, he felt different. It was as if he was in possession of something he had thought lost. He had found a coin in his pocket that had been escaping his reach for a long time.

A cold rain had its fingers on the land the next day. The wind was sharp. Winter whistled through the air.

"Seasons are changing," Rufus said as he came in at noon and stood by the fire to warm himself.

"There'll be a month of good days before the cold weather settles down," Jennet assured him, thinking of all she wanted to do and how the time would scarcely be long enough.

Danny was open-mouthed and wide-eyed at the stories they told him of the winter, for it was little of it that he had ever seen. Dampness, yes, and cold, and the family drawing close to the smouldering peat fire when storm swept the hills and rain lashed against the windows. "Sure and there are ways of beating the weather," he said as he thought of a winter's night in Donegal.

That evening after darkness closed in, giving the safety needed for Danny to come downstairs and be a part of the Austin family, the rain froze as it fell and the world outside was soon glazed with ice; but inside there was cheer and warmth as they sat by the hearth. Jennet was weaving at her loom and the young people were telling stories. When the blaze of the fire had gone down to coals, they let it sink to ash; for the room was warm and held the heat well.

Rufus fetched a jar of popcorn from the shelf and held it before Danny. "Ever seen the like of that?" he asked.

"Sure and it's seed you'll put in the ground next April."

Rufus shook his head.

"Sure then and it's what you'll give your hens to make the yolks of the eggs a fine color."

Rufus went on shaking his head. Benoni buried his face in his hands to hide the laughter creeping over it. Even Melody was smiling–half in amazement, half in pity at Danny's consternation.

"You shall soon see, then," Rufus said, "but I hope it won't give you such a fright that you'll jump out of your shirt."

"*Your* shirt," Danny reminded him. "Ah well, it's as easy as an old shoe on me, but I think I'll not readily part company with it."

Rufus winked at his brother. "Come along, Ben."

The two boys approached the hearth with the jar of corn and each one took a handful. Carefully they buried the kernels, here and there throughout the warm white ash. Jennet left her weaving to join in the fun, and Melody clasped her hands together to contain her excitement. Rufus and Benoni stepped away from the hearth and tried to appear as if nothing unusual were about to take place. Danny looked from one to another, but neither by word nor gesture would anyone indicate what might happen.

There was a stirring and quivering in the ash, followed by a series of tiny explosions. Suddenly one white-winged ball and then another shot out into the room. The barrage increased until the room was almost like a snowstorm and the white caps were lying everywhere. Some made only a dull plop and rolled just onto the edge of the hearth bricks; some went straight up into the air and Melody and the boys caught them in their hands; others shot across the room to land on the loom or the bed in the far corner. Danny watched the rain of white pellets in utter amazement, while Melody and Jennet raced around the room picking them up and putting them in a bowl which they placed on the table.

"If that's not magic, my name's not O'Dare!"

Rufus wanted to scoop up a handful and eat, but Jennet made him wait until she had brought butter from the cool room and salt from her stores; then she shook the bowl and shook it until golden runnels of butter had covered the white caps and salt glistened on them. She passed the bowl around–to Danny first, telling him to take his hands full, and last to Melody, while Rufus tucked more corn in the ash so that they would not lack a second round.

When the next shower started through the room, Danny joined in catching the white caps with the others. They made a game of it this time, seeing how many they could catch in the air, how many they could recover from the far corners of the room. They were laughing and making so much noise that none of them heard the repeated, impatient knocking on the door. Melody was aware of it before the others. She ran to Jennet and placed her hands on her mother's shoulders, then on her lips; she ran to Danny and forced him down behind the loom.

"What is it?" Rufus asked, his mouth full of popcorn.

"Someone at the door," Jennet answered hoarsely.

"Can we get Danny upstairs?"

"It's too late now. He's safe behind the loom. Benoni, move those blankets–so," Jennet whispered. "There, that's better. Rufus, put a log on the fire." She started across the room toward the door. "Whoever's there, I'm coming," she called out. Then she lifted the latch. "Why, Deacon Phillips!" she exclaimed in surprise. "Come in."

"Such merrymaking I've never heard short of Christmas," Deacon Phillips said gruffly, stepping inside while Jennet closed the door behind him. "Where's Jared?"

"Over the mountain. He'll not be back for two more nights."

Deacon Phillips brought his riding whip across his boot with a thud. "And he's got the best horse around here!"

Rufus looked up from the fire. "What is it, sir, the Hue and Cry called out again?"

"Yes. A white mare has been stolen from two townships to the north of here, heading south they say. She was kept in hiding today, but tracks have been seen and galloping hoofs have been heard. She'll be easy to mark on a night like this. But it's a bad night."

"Snow?"

"Not yet. Ice is filming the roads. It calls for a clever man on a clever horse. I thought to go down the turnpike and block the crossroads. I wanted Jared to head toward the bridge. He and Pepper could do it."

"But, sir, I–" Rufus began quickly.

Jennet stepped forward between Rufus and Deacon Phillips. "Rufus is as clever with a horse as his father," she replied proudly.

"I know, I know," Deacon Phillips wagged his head and kept thumping his whip across his boot. "But if Jared is away with Pepper, I wouldn't try another horse." He looked up quickly. "Willow's in foal, isn't she? You wouldn't want to run her on a night like this. And Midnight isn't smart enough."

"Is there a reward?" Rufus asked.

Deacon Phillips shook his head. "The mare's well bred, but the schoolteacher to whom she belongs had no money to post a reward, and our Hue and Cry is so short of funds that we can't post one for him. It's the honor, my lad. We can't let another horse thief get through our township."

"But, sir, I–" Rufus was eager to ride in pursuit.

Jennet interrupted. "Either of the boys could do it."

"A rider is only half the story; it's the horse that matters more tonight," Deacon Phillips turned to face the door. "I'll be going. If I'm in luck, I'll head the thief off at the crossroads and apprehend him myself. Good night to you."

"Won't you have something warm before you go? Some popcorn? Some–" Jennet began.

"No, no," his hands were on the latch. "I've no time for frivolity on a night like this." He opened the door quickly.

Jennet caught a glimpse of his horse standing with dropping head and bedraggled tail as the icy rain-laden wind swirled about him. She watched Deacon Phillips mount and ride off before she closed the door.

"Mother," Rufus blurted out, "why did you keep stopping me? Why didn't you tell him that we had Pepper in the barn?"

Jennet laid her hand on Rufus. "Your father left Pepper here for Danny in case Blue is discovered and Danny should have to flee."

"Pepper for Danny?" Rufus was incredulous. "But Pepper is father's horse and the best horse we have. We couldn't get on without Pepper."

"I know, Rufus, but your father thought Danny couldn't get on without a horse."

Danny came out from behind the loom and joined them. A few weeks ago he had been bewildered by unkindness;

now he was bewildered by kindness. "I don't understand," he said. "What is this talk about a horse for me?"

"If you need to escape, Jared wants you to have the means at hand," Jennet explained quietly. "He's left Pepper for you."

"For me to use?"

"As your own."

"My—own?"

"Mother!" Rufus exclaimed. "Danny would be picked up as a thief if he were found in any township within forty miles on Pepper. Pepper is too well known as father's horse."

"Jared left something for Danny," Jennet said as she clapped her hands and gestured to Melody to go to the fire-place cupboard and bring her the Bible. Melody did as her mother requested. Jennet took from within the book a few papers folded together.

"That's not it," she said, as she unfolded the handbill that described Blue Lightning's loss and reward. "Nor that." She unfolded the paper telling about the school in Connecticut. Then she unfolded a blank sheet of paper, scrutinized it carefully, nodded, and handed it to Danny. "This gives you Pepper as your own," she said.

He laughed. This was a strange land where people gave deeds with no writing on them. "It says nothing."

"That's for your own good," Jennet replied. "If you need to have the paper speak, hold it to the fire. If you have no need, you are better off with no written words on you to say your name and give others information they've no business to know."

Danny, with the paper in his hands, crossed the room to the hearth. He knelt down on the bricks and held the paper to the heat. The paper quivered, contracting a little; then the shape of words appeared on it. They were words clearly written in a hand well known to those who stood behind the Irish boy and read as he read:

I, Jared Austin, do, by this deed, give forever into the keeping of Daniel O'Dare my brown gelding Pepper: to do with as he likes, to go with where he wishes, and to care for as if Pepper were his own.

Jared Austin

Under the last line, Jared had drawn a design of flowers that might have been a plan for the patterns he would someday put upon a bare wall.

Jennet saw the design almost more than the words. "It's Jared who knows that good often will flower if it's given the chance," she murmured.

Danny sat back on his thighs; and as he withdrew the paper from the heat, the words faded until they disappeared. Then he folded the paper and put it in his pocket. He put his head in his hands as if he were praying. "I'm not worthy," he whispered over and over.

Jennet knew why he had covered his eyes. A man had his own pride, especially when other men were present. "Jared thinks you are, or he would not have done it," she said in a low voice.

Melody knelt down on the hearth beside Danny and put both hands on his shoulders, compelling him to look at her. "Dan," she said his name awkwardly, harshly; then she put her hands on her heart.

"I know," he said, nodding his head. "You all trust me. Would to God that I could do something to make myself worthy of your trust, to prove to you that I'm half the man you think me to be."

Melody dropped her hands, and her gaze turned toward the fire.

Danny looked into the leaping flames as if he would see in them some answer to the longing that was in him. After a moment he got up quickly and stood facing Rufus who was leaning against the mantel. "If Pepper is mine, I've a mind to ride him tonight."

"Tonight!" Rufus exclaimed.

"Aye, tonight."

Rufus and Benoni stared at the Irish lad, their eyes troubled and questioning.

"It's a bad night for a horse and worse for a rider," Rufus said, irritation edging his tongue, "but for a man who wants to evade the law it may be as good a night as any with the countryside searching for a white horse."

"Don't follow the turnpike to the crossroads or you'll ride straight into Deacon Phillips's hands," Benoni warned.

"It's not for myself I'll ride tonight," Danny said, "but in pursuit of a fine white mare and, please God, I'll not come back till I've found her."

"Danny!" Rufus shouted. "You mean you'll do the work of the Hue and Cry?"

"That's what I mean." Danny smiled gaily. Such a short time ago the cruelty of one man had made him bitter against the world; now the kindness of one man made him want to brave the world in derring-do.

"But you don't know the roads!"

"You can tell me what ones to take, Rufus, and they'll not be unfamiliar to Pepper."

"If anyone rides tonight, I should be the one," Rufus said.

Danny reached out to clasp Rufus's hand. "I'll thank you for giving me the honor, for it's what I'm needing more than you."

The gesture warmed Rufus and his voice softened as he spoke to Danny. "I'd not want you to get into any trouble, Danny."

"And what trouble could I get into if Pepper is mine to ride where I will?"

Rufus, with no ready answer of his own, looked toward his mother.

"I think we should let Danny do what he wants to do, Rufus," Jennet said.

Danny turned to her and took her hand in his, pressing it impulsively to his lips. "Thank you for those words, my lady, for there's a feeling strong within me that I may find the white mare tonight." Then he rolled back his head and laughed. "And if I don't–"

"You'll come back to us," Jennet reminded him.

"Indeed and I'll do that."

"Pepper will know the way home," Benoni said, "if the darkness and the turnings confuse you."

"It won't be the first time I've put myself in the care of a horse."

"Mother," Rufus demanded, "why shouldn't I ride with Danny?"

"Not tonight, Rufus," Jennet said firmly. "It would do Willow no good."

Danny turned to Benoni. "My saddle on Pepper and the bridle I used on Blue Lightning will fit well enough." He turned to Rufus. "I'll thank you for the loan of a coat against the cold, for I've naught but this shirt and it's seen better days."

Benoni left the room and went to the barn. Rufus went upstairs. Melody looked at her mother and Danny, knowing Danny had said something that was pleasing them all.

"Oh, Danny," Jennet said turning to him, "have a care. It's a wicked night."

Danny seemed to have grown an inch as he stood by the fire, and the look on his face was the look of a man who has glimpsed the work he can do in the world. "We've a saying in Donegal that the angels of the Lord care for the man who casts care to the winds." He leaned toward Jennet and kissed her quickly; then he went to the door.

Rufus was standing there holding a coat and a cap in his hands. Danny thrust his arms into the coat and buttoned it. The cap he put on his head. Together they went out into the wind and the rain.

Melody stood before her mother. She put her hands to her eyes; then she described a circle with her hands, closing it as she placed her hands over her heart. Jennet's eyes filled with tears as she saw the smile on the girl's face.

"Oh, my dear daughter, you're not the only one," she said as she held out her arms to enfold Melody. "I don't know what he's done, but he's made us all love him." There were times when Jennet spoke to Melody as if she could hear the words on her lips.

Chapter Ten

Danny mounted Pepper in the barnyard and settled himself in the saddle. Benoni swung the gate open. Rufus held the lamp high, but the glow was a small one in the wildness of the night. There was little enough to reflect its gleam except the eyes of the horse and those of the boy as he leaned low over Pepper's neck and spoke persuasively to him. Pepper took a prancing step or two as if to show his readiness, but Danny gathered the reins in and held him back. He turned to the two boys standing near. Rufus would have exchanged places with him in a moment, but Benoni was glad he was not the one to be riding on such a night.

"Follow the road south for some two miles," Rufus said, raising his voice so that the wind and the rain would not carry his words away. "When you come to a fork, bear right or you'll find yourself on the turnpike and that's where the deacon has gone."

Danny accepted the directions, knowing they would guide him over the first part of the way. "Tell me," he asked; "is it north of your field that the Phillips farm lies?"

Rufus nodded.

Danny smiled. "I'm hoping that when the deacon goes out to water his stock in the light of morning, he'll see a white horse in one of his stalls."

"He'll thank you for it if he does."

"I want no thanks," Danny said. "All I want is to see a horse returned to its owner."

"That's the spirit of the Hue and Cry," Rufus commented.

Pepper lifted a front hoof and pawed the ground. He knew something lay ahead of him, and he was restive.

"Easy there, my treasure," Danny crooned. "We'll go in good time." He looked at the two boys. "It's leaving you I am," he said; then he touched his heels to Pepper's sides, released the reins, and the horse shot forward.

Rufus held the lantern as high as he could reach, but horse and rider went quickly beyond its beam. The thud of hoofs on the ice-tipped grass of the yard could be heard; then the sound changed as the horse turned onto the road. Iron shoes hit against stones and rang dully against the storm-whipped night.

Danny leaned over Pepper's neck, keeping up a steady flow of talk to hearten the horse. He had not gone fifty paces from the house without realizing the dangers of the night, for Pepper's legs were sliding out from under him. There were places in the road where hoofs could get little purchase, and there were other places where the ground was only crusted with ice and the danger of slipping was less.

Straining his eyes ahead, Danny tried to see the best of the road for the horse. Soon his eyes grew more accustomed to the darkness. He peered before him, one cheek laid against Pepper's mane, the other stung by the icy wind. His hands, resting surely on the reins, were ready to bring Pepper to a halt or loose him into the fullness of his stride.

Now he could see the road for a horse length ahead of him and that was enough to steer Pepper away from stones and treacherous places. He kept to the soft center of the road when he could, for it was quicker traveling than the grass-grown side, but there was one advantage to the grass: it dulled the sound of his hoofbeats. His ears strained into the darkness almost as much as his eyes; another echoing of hoofs, a cough, heavy breathing, any one of a dozen sounds might give him a clue.

He followed Rufus's directions to the fork. He had been following a set of hoofprints as well, but these had been made by Deacon Phillips's horse traveling over the road a quarter hour before him. He had felt sure of that, for they were newly made. The rain had not filled them, and when it was time for him to leave the road, they went on to the crossroads ahead. At the fork he parted company with the hoofprints almost as he would have parted company with a companion. Now he was on the road that led to the bridge, and it had not been recently traveled he was sure, for there were no hoofprints to be easily seen.

His eyes pierced the darkness as he drew Pepper in to a halt. He dismounted to feel the road surface, to confirm what his sight told him. Nothing had passed that way within the hour, for the streaming icy rain had obliterated all but the ruts that were worn deep in the road. But this was one of the ways the thief might have run. He could have passed over it earlier and be in hiding somewhere. Danny looked around him, though he could not penetrate the black veil of the night. The thief might be hiding in the darkness of the woods, wet as they were; or he might be taking shelter in some barn just off the road. If he were that near, the white horse might neigh to Pepper and so give his rider away.

Danny mounted and urged Pepper on. "Aroon, aroon," he whispered to the horse. "It's you I'm depending on now, and not on your legs alone. If there's one of your kind hiding within this world of darkness, call out to him in your own way."

They trotted through the night until they came to the crest of a long hill that fell from them into a void of uncertainty. Danny reined Pepper in and held him to a walk as he picked his way carefully down the incline. At the bottom a bridge presented an obstacle, for ice had formed on the wood. Danny got off and tied Pepper loosely to a tree while he examined the bridge. There would be no crossing it on a horse that night. Legs would splay out helplessly on the slippery surface, and there was nothing to keep a horse from going over the unrailed side to the brook running below.

Danny could not keep his own legs under him on the bridge; so he laid himself flat on the slippery surface and crossed it as if he were swimming, arms and legs working together. His eyes were a few inches above the ice. Suddenly he caught his breath. There were tracks beneath the ice: tracks made in the soft slush perhaps an hour ago, which the glaze of ice had covered. They were heading southwest, the way he was traveling. Rufus had told him the road was a lonely piece after the bridge with no clearings or houses, only thick woodland on either side. Six miles beyond the bridge lay a meeting of roads and an inn.

Danny drew his knees under him and lifted his head into the icy night. He took off his cap and clasped his hands together. "God in heaven," he said aloud, "lead me right."

He was trembling as he crawled back across the bridge to where Pepper stood, trembling not from cold but from the possibility before him. He led Pepper down the steep bank and along the brook till he found a place where they both could cross. Danny plunged into the water first, holding Pepper's reins. He would not trust the horse to try the brook bed until he had tested it for safety. The water was cold and up to his thighs. When he gained the other side, he pulled on the reins and spoke to the horse, who followed him carefully. Once on the road again he mounted and pressed Pepper into a fast trot.

The shelter of woodland had given some protection to the road and the rain had not beat so hard on it. Here and there the prints of hoofs were evident, and they were those of a running horse. It might be the white mare. Indeed, it was the white mare, Danny thought to himself, for who else would be out on a night like this? And who but someone fleeing would want to run a horse with the danger there was to life and limb?

Pepper was breathing hard, and Danny was panting with eagerness when the warm glow of light from the inn held out its beckoning hand to them. Even at that hour, the inn was lively, filled with drovers, teamsters, and journeymen seeking refuge for the night and a shelter for their animals.

Danny led Pepper into a shed where three teams were tied. The horses whinnied to each other. Danny fastened Pepper and loosened his saddle girth; then he went toward the inn. He felt in his pocket for the piece of paper that had given him his horse. To have a horse in his own name was to be a man among men. He squared his shoulders and held his head high as he went toward the door.

There was so much talk going on among the group by the hearth that no one heard the door open. Danny shut it behind him quietly and stood in the doorway looking at the people who occupied the room. The innkeeper was bending over a kettle of cider on the hearth, and his wife stood beside him with a tray of cups. On the bench facing the fire were three hearty fellows whose clothes looked as if they had taken a drenching but were fast drying in the blaze and the heat. At the table a man sat whittling. He was a drover by his looks, Danny thought, working on a new goad for his oxen, since the one he had used that day had perhaps been broken when he slipped on the ice.

A short distance from the fire stood a settle, and on it sat a young man with a book in his hands. He was the only one to look up when the door opened. His eyes and Danny's met–above the noise and steam, above the merriment–but he dropped his glance first. Danny kept staring at him. His clothes were wet, but he was not trying to dry them as the others were. He was keeping away from people for reasons of his own. Danny stepped nearer to see the man better. The inner part of his trousers was dry, as if his legs had been held close to the sides of a horse.

The innkeeper turned quickly. "Here's another traveler," he said at sight of Danny.

His wife looked up from the tray of cups. "Welcome, stranger. A wild night it is."

"It is so indeed," Danny replied as he crossed toward the hearth.

Shouts of welcome and loud greetings came to him from the teamsters and the drover, but no word of any kind came from the man on the settle with the book in his hands.

Danny took one of the cups the woman offered him. "Here's life to you all," he said, "and good cheer on the wings of the morning." He clapped the innkeeper on his back.

The man on the bench laughed. "You're not from these parts with words like that."

Danny laughed. "You're right, my friend. I'm from over the sea, and I'm on my way to a fortune, for I've heard tell you've got them in this land."

The men laughed and made a place for him on the bench.

"Is your horse bedded, stranger?"

"Tied with the teams in the shed."

"You're the first man to ride in this night," the innkeeper said.

"The first!" Danny exclaimed, his eyes roving to the man on the settle. "Well, my horse should have the best if he's that brave."

"And the best hay he shall have as soon as we've drained our cups."

"It's no hay my horse wants," Danny said, "but a drink of cider if you've some to spare."

"Cider!"

"Sure and that's what he's had since he was weaned."

The innkeeper stirred the iron kettle of cider. "The horse that drinks cider can have it free," he said.

"Drink it! He'll go down on his knees and thank you for it in words like my own."

"A talking horse!" the man exclaimed, while the innkeeper looked at Danny with incredulous eyes.

Danny raised his cup to his lips and emptied it; then he set it back on the tray and sat down on the long bench. "See for yourselves," he said, "but tell him to leave a drop for me, or we'll have words on the morrow."

The innkeeper poured the hot cider into a copper basin and started out of the kitchen, followed by his wife, the teamsters and the drover, all eager to see and hear for themselves the marvel of a talking horse.

"And if he doesn't talk right away, give him some more and wait to hear what he says," Danny called after them, "but don't hold it against me if he shames you!"

One after another they left the kitchen, all save the man who sat on the settle and Danny, whose eyes were on the man.

When the door was shut, Danny crossed quickly toward the man. Standing before him he placed his hands on his shoulders and let the strength of his fingers curl round the bone. "Tell me now, before they come back, where you have left the white mare, for I'm seeking her and I've no time to lose."

The man struggled to free himself from Danny's grip. "You heard it said that you were the first to ride in on a horse this night," he muttered.

"How came you then; by carriage?" Danny asked.

The man shook his head. "Nay, I was a walker in the night."

"A man walking on a night like this won't keep the inside of his legs as dry as yours are. Come now, speak quick and tell me what I want to know."

"I–" the man began, then paused.

"Speak up, man, or I'll shake you till your bones rattle like a skeleton and your teeth fly about the room like popcorn escaping the heat of the fire."

The man shook his head. "I haven't any horse."

"Not one of your own, I'll warrant, but one you've helped yourself to for reasons of your own. Out with it now. I've not been following you down the road for nothing."

"Was it your hoofbeats I heard behind me?"

"It was, if it wasn't your own heart beating in terror."

There had been silence in the room after the others went out, but now their voices could be heard as they left the shed and drew near the kitchen. Boisterous and angry the tone was, not jovial and wondering as when they had gone out.

"Quick now," Danny said, and the man winced at the hold on his neck.

"I had to get away." The man breathed hard.

"Like as not, but I'll thank you for telling me where the white mare is."

The man was choking now and his eyes were rolling.

"Behind the wood–" Then he let out a scream as the others could be heard at the door. "Help, I'm being murdered!"

The innkeeper burst into the room. Danny released his hold and turned around to face him. The man squirmed on the settle and put his hand up to his throat as if to assure himself it was still of a piece.

"What is going on?" the innkeeper demanded. "Isn't there trouble enough outside without bringing it in?"

Danny smiled engagingly. "Sure and he's riding a horse not his own, and I'm only asking him where it is that he's tied it."

"A pretty tale and you expect me to believe it!"

The teamsters and the drover crowded through the open door into the room.

"If he's a thief, you're a liar!" the innkeeper roared. "I'd like to throw you both out into the night. What do you mean by saying your horse would drink cider? Making a fool of me, are you?" He held up the copper basin, still full with warm liquid.

"Poor beast! The bad night has got him so fuddled he doesn't know what's good. Bring the cider to me and see if I'll refuse it."

The innkeeper glared at him. "You'll have nothing from me except the feel of my right arm until you tell me what you are doing with Jared Austin's horse."

"He's a thief, not me," the man on the settle screamed. "Throw him out into the night and let him see what it feels like to walk as I've been doing!"

The men gathered angrily around Danny, their faces that had once been pleasant now hard and threatening. The innkeeper's wife came in the door with an armful of wood, and the man on the settle went toward the door to help her. The men, menacing and demanding explanations, strode toward Danny. He wanted to make a dash for the open door, but the space between was blocked; so he stood tall above them instead.

"Jared Austin's horse is mine, and I can prove it if you'll let me."

"Thief!" the innkeeper lunged at Danny.

Danny ducked his head to avoid the blow.

"Liar!" the drover shouted.

Danny leaped back, trying to dodge their blows. His actions enraged them and they closed in on him until they had overpowered him. They rolled him over on the floor and tied him up, then went through his pockets to find some evidence. All they found was a sheet of folded paper. The innkeeper unfolded it, and while he turned it inside out and back again in search of some writing there was silence in the room.

"If you'll let me explain," Danny said, "that paper gives me my right to Jared Austin's Pepper."

"Quiet!" the innkeeper demanded.

The fire was crackling on the hearth. The rain was spitting against the windows. The men were breathing heavily. The woman sighed to herself. Then a new sound broke across the silence. It was the pounding of a horse's hoofs echoing through the night.

"Who is riding so hard on a night like this?" The innkeeper looked up from the paper he held in his hands.

"Whoever it is is not coming but going," his wife said, standing near the door and opening it a crack. She put her head out then turned back quickly. "It's the odd man! He's on a white horse, and he's the one who said he was a walker in the night!"

Danny struggled on the floor in his bonds. "What direction is he taking?" he called out.

So compelling was his tone that the woman opened the door again and peered out, but the sound of running hoofs was lost in the bitter laughter of the innkeeper.

"Two thiefs in a night? One has escaped us, but the other is trussed like a fowl for the spit. Not bad for ice and snow!" He crumpled the paper in his hands and tossed it into the fire.

"Look! Look! For the love of heaven, look!" Danny cried. His voice was the only pointer he had, and he directed it toward the flame.

The innkeeper turned his head quickly, thinking something had caught fire. He reached for the poker to push the big log back and at that moment the white paper flattened itself across the log and the intense heat made the writing visible. Out of the flame and from the rapidly disintegrating paper a handful of words gave fiery evidence–

Do . . . give forever . . . of Daniel O'Dare . . . gelding Pepper . . . as if . . . his own

Then the paper sailed up the chimney carrying Jared's name with it, but the bottom line with the tracery of flowers did not burn. Breaking away, it fell from the fire onto the hearth where it lay quivering and smoking.

"There's only one man in all this countryside who can draw flowers like that," the innkeeper said. "That's Jared Austin's mark, and it's as good a bond as his name." He turned to the teamsters and the drover. "Unhand him, men. The horse is his, though how or why, we've lost our chance of knowing."

"He gave the horse to me because he thought I might need a horse," Danny explained, "and if what your ears tell you is true, it's a night when any man who can ride needs a horse."

They rolled Danny over and cut the knots they had tied, unwinding the cords that lashed his limbs. Danny stretched his legs and arms; then he sprang to his feet and leaped across the room to stand beside the woman.

"Can you tell us where he went?" he asked, earnest and eager.

"He took the river road as sure as I've eyes in my head."

Danny faced the men. "To your horses, men! The Hue and Cry has work to do this night. It's a white mare we're seeking, and we'll find her sure."

With a shout of union, the men forgot their animosity of a few moments earlier and followed Danny out into the night. Pepper needed only to be untied and to have his girth tightened. Soon Danny was in the saddle, cantering down the road which the woman had pointed out. It was not hard for Danny to see that he was following another horse, for the icy rain had had no time to fill in where pounding hoofs had broken the surface.

The innkeeper came fast behind Danny on his own powerful stallion. The teamsters followed, riding bareback on their heavy horses as soon as they had disengaged them from the wagons. In a matter of minutes, five horses were racing down the road and the sound of their hoofs in the night was more than the sound of the storm. The innkeeper rode close behind Danny on the grassy side of the road where there was less danger of slipping.

Danny, his head strained forward, caught the sound of hoofs in the distance. Pepper ran well, so quick was he to catch the urgency of the chase.

"Where does the road go?" Danny shouted to the man behind him.

"It's ten miles to the Massachusetts border," the innkeeper roared, "but there's a bridge to cross before we've gone three miles."

"What kind of bridge?" Danny turned his head and spat his words into the night to make them carry.

"A long bridge and the river beneath it is deep; an open bridge."

Danny held Pepper back so that the other man might come alongside him. "If he tries to run the mare over the bridge, he'll break her legs on the ice."

"If he tries to ford the river, he'll meet sand that will mire the mare."

They passed on. Ahead of him Danny could see the shape of a white horse in the night and the dark form of a rider bent low on her back as if he had given himself to the animal and cared little where she went.

"Steer them away from the bridge," the innkeeper shouted.

Danny, who had held Pepper in rein, released his hold as he had more than once on the turf when the winning post came into view. It was the signal to use that reserve of speed which Danny knew the horse still harbored. Pepper shot ahead, and Danny guided him until they were neck and neck with the white mare and then ahead of her. The road was ice-covered, but so fast and hard were they going that iron shoes broke easily through the crust.

"Now, my treasure," Danny whispered, "your heart and your legs and your soul." The bridge was ahead, not more than the length of two horses. Danny swerved Pepper so that the road was blocked.

The white mare snorted and jumped sideways, parting company with her rider. She fell to her knees, then rolled over the high shoulder of the road and landed in the sand near the river's edge. Pepper, turning shortly, hit the ice-covered planks of the bridge with a hind leg. He slipped, but regained his stance without going down. Danny kicked his feet free of the stirrups and jumped to the ground, letting the reins lie on Pepper's neck.

"Well done, my lovely," he whispered as he put his arms around his horse.

Pepper stood heaving and panting, stretching his neck out.

The innkeeper reined in his horse, slid from his saddle, and leaped over the embankment to grasp the dangling reins of the white mare and urge her out of the sand. The teamsters arrived on their heavy horses, and seeing what was needed, dismounted quickly. One of them gathered in the reins of the standing horses and held them while the two others joined the innkeeper in his attempt to free the mare. Choosing their positions so that they would avoid any suction from the sand, one teamster laid his hand on the mare's left flank, and the other laid a hand on her right flank, while the innkeeper pulled on her reins. Shouting and cheering, they urged her to make the effort by which she could free herself.

The mare heaved and snorted; then with a tremendous effort she pulled herself out of the mire. Once on firm ground, she shook herself vigorously and whinnied in greeting to the five horses that stood near. Each man in turn, beginning with the innkeeper and ending with Danny, felt the mare with practiced hands. As far as they could tell in the darkness of the night and the noise of the storm, she was sound in every limb, and no harm had been done her.

"When the mud is washed off her," the innkeeper said, "even her own master will know her." He looked around him. "Where's the rider?"

Everyone turned and peered into the night. The teamsters hallooed in great echoing voices, but the man was gone.

"He's off into the night on his own legs this time," one of the teamsters said.

"A walker he is now, for sure."

"Nay, a runner," the innkeeper remarked, "for he'll put all the distance he can between himself and us, thinking we may carry on with the chase."

"I'd not want to take the horses across that bridge," one of the teamsters said.

The innkeeper nodded in agreement. "I've not the heart to pursue a man on a night like this–and the horse we have."

"Poor fellow," Danny murmured, looking into the darkness.

"Mayhap he'll meet a better kind of justice in the night than he'd meet if we turned him over to the sheriff," one of the teamsters commented.

"Mayhap," Danny agreed. He turned and mounted Pepper, leading the white mare beside him. "She's a fine horse for a schoolmaster to own," he remarked.

"You know the mare then?"

"In a manner of speaking, yes; and I'll lead her along with me, for I know where she bides tonight."

The innkeeper smiled at Danny. "We'll ride as far as the inn together, and you shall have what you wish to warm you against your journey."

During the night the storm wore itself out. The first streak of morning light revealed a sodden world, crusted with ice. Hard surfaces like the sides of buildings and stone walls were glazed; many trees were bowed low by the weight on leaves and twigs; but the softer surfaces of fields and pastures were wet and rain-soaked.

Deacon Phillips, who had returned to his house late, cold, and empty-handed, had gone to bed reluctantly. As leader of the Hue and Cry for the past year, he had been proud of the reputation of his township, but now within a month two horse thieves had escaped their net, and he felt a personal responsibility. He slept soundly once he got into bed. When he awoke, it was to blink his eyes and look around him in sleep-heavy bewilderment, for it was not the light that had aroused him. It was something else. Only the merest crack of light was coming in through the drawn curtains.

He felt his attention quickening as his mind weighed possibilities. Then he heard a sound that was unmistakable to him, though it might have gone unrecognized by many. It was the thudding of a horse's hoofs. The white mare, he thought, for who else would be abroad on such a morning? Leaping from his bed, he crossed the room quickly to the window.

But it was no white mare he saw, only the hind quarters of Jared Austin's Pepper going slowly down the road. Deacon Phillips's heart sank within him, and he scratched his head in puzzlement. It was an odd time for Jared to be returning from his work; but then Jared, next to being the best neighbor a man could have, was an odd person. For many an activity, night was the same as day to him. Deacon Phillips sighed. Had Jared been back a few hours earlier, the stolen mare might be in her own stable now.

The deacon leaned forward and stared, eyes intent. The road was not smooth as it should have been after a night of rain and frost. It was churned with the marks of more than one horse. His eyes followed the hoofprints, and he went quickly to the corner window of his room to see them better. They led across the yard to his barn, and then away again. Muttering to himself, he pulled his boots on and went to the barn. His own horse whinnied as he entered, and the work team joined in, but there was another voice too, unfamiliar and impatient.

Deacon Phillips approached the box stall that was always kept in readiness for a traveler's horse. The sight he saw made him smile, and the smile gave to his face a look like that of the rising sun.

There stood a white mare, eating hay from the manger and whinnying between mouthfuls. Her coat had been rubbed down. Her mane and tail had been combed. There was no mud spattering her legs or underbelly. Except that she had drunk well of the bucket of water in a corner of the stall and eaten half the hay in the manger, there was no evidence of her having been ridden hard through a night of wind and storm.

The deacon stood beside the horse, shaking his head and smiling. Jared must have returned shortly after his call at the Austin house; then Jennet had told him what was wanted and Jared had headed the thief off at the bridge. Deacon Phillips slapped his hands on his thighs. It had been a toss-up with him whether the bridge or the turnpike crossroads would be the place to catch the thief, but he was glad that Jared had won out. Too bad there was no reward, for Jared Austin was one who saw little money and could use plenty, but the gratitude of the schoolmaster at having his mare back and the honor of the township were rewards in their way.

"How was it I slept so sound?" the Deacon muttered; then he remembered the noise of the storm, as wind fought against rain and both raged over the land.

Back at the Austin barn, Danny put Pepper in his stall and took off the saddle and bridle. He rubbed the horse down well and bathed his legs, then wiped his saddle with a cloth and left it upturned to dry from the underside. He made a small amount of wet mash for Pepper, and the horse whinnied eagerly as Danny set it before him. Pepper had known Jared's hands on him for years past, but he recognized a kindred touch in Danny's.

Another nicker sounded in the barn and Danny went to the stall where Blue Lightning stood. He fondled the horse's head in greeting, then instinctively felt his legs. He was pleased at Blue's condition, but he looked on the horse with different eyes since Pepper had been given to him. He owed a debt of kindness to Jared Austin, a debt that could only be repaid by returning Blue Lightning to Captain Isaac Mallow.

Danny leaned against the horse and thought how it was possible now for him to repay that debt: possible because he was becoming an honest man.

"I'll be after you soon," he whispered into Blue's ear before he left the barn.

When Danny crossed the space from barn to house, he saw the first blue spiral of smoke coming from the chimney. Jennet had stirred life into the fire and swung the kettle of porridge over the heat. He was hungry. Warmth would feel good too, though his clothes that had been soaked through earlier in the night had gradually been drying on him.

All the family members were gathered by the hearth, and they greeted Danny with gladness. The Irish boy, whose heart had been hungering ever since he had left his own home, realized that their praise and delight meant as much to him as the fire and the bowl of porridge Jennet placed in his hands. He told them of all he had done.

"But, Danny, why didn't you wake Deacon Phillips?" Rufus asked. "He would have been that pleased to see you and hear of your deeds from your own lips."

Danny stared. "Arra, but I'm still a hunted man! My face and my voice would have given me away."

Jennet shook her head, and the smile waned from her lips. Danny's intentions might be good enough now, but the fact remained that he had done wrong and must some time face the consequences.

Danny turned toward her. "I'm thinking I'll take Blue Lightning back to his owner."

"Danny!" Rufus and Benoni exclaimed together.

"But I'd like not to give myself to the sheriff, for if I did it might bring trouble to you for your kindness to me."

"Jared would have something to say, Danny, if he were here," Jennet said, looking up at the boy. "All I know is that there's no right way to do a wrong thing. It was wrong to take Blue Lightning, but you can make amends by returning him."

She looked away, for her eyes had suddenly filled with tears. Ever since Danny had appeared in their midst she had known Blue Lightning must some day be returned to his owner, and that until he was they all lived in danger. Jared had been sure that Danny would do it of his own free will. Jennet's heart reached out in longing for Jared's presence in their midst. She brushed her hand across her eyes.

"I wish Jared were here to see you go. Couldn't you wait for him, Danny? He'll be back tomorrow."

Danny shook his head. There was more in his heart than he could say in words, but the experience of the previous night when he had acted in accordance with the law made him feel for the first time as if he belonged to the new land. He wanted to be worthy of belonging, and he could not be so as long as he knew himself to be a thief.

"Blue's leg is good now," Benoni said, "just as good as the other three."

"And the dye is holding," Jennet added, proud of her mixture. "Until sweat or rain drive it out, he's a black horse to all who see him."

"Then I'll ride with him today to the seaport town and return him to his owner." Danny's voice was strong with decision.

Silence fell on them all at the thought that Danny would soon be leaving them, and with none of them was there any sure knowing as to when he would be back with them again. Danny sat down on the settle beside Melody and wrote quickly on her slate. A shadow passed over her face as she realized that he was going away. She took the chalk from him and drew the outline of a bird. Danny was puzzled. He glanced up at Benoni who was standing near them.

"It's the cuckoo," Benoni said. "No other bird wears whiskers."

Melody opened her mouth and gave the bird's call.

"What does she mean?" Benoni asked.

"I'm not sure."

Melody was shaping words with her mouth. "Muck-a-wiss." The effort was a costly one, but she smiled happily after she had made it.

Then Danny smiled. He knew what she meant, and he nodded vigorously. Putting one hand on his heart to show that he was in earnest, he wrote with the other on her slate. "I'll come back to you."

Melody reached toward him and took both his hands in hers.

Rufus came over to stand beside them. Melody looked up at him and held three fingers of one hand up to Rufus, then smiled broadly.

"She has three brothers now," Rufus said, "and she wants you to know that you belong here with us."

Danny nodded. "Three brothers, and the third is coming back in three days. I'll be walking then, but I'm thinking I'll be an honest man."

"If you give the horse up yourself, who's to have the reward?" Rufus said quickly. "Why shouldn't I go along with you and be the one to receive it?"

"Why not indeed!" Danny exclaimed. "And when two travel together, one shortens the road for the other."

Jennet looked startled. "But they'll jail you, Danny."

"Will they now?" he asked, rolling his eyes roguishly.

"Oh, Mother," Rufus said, "I think Captain Mallow will be so glad to have his stallion returned by the man who took him that he'll not think of punishment."

Jennet's expression was one of hope shadowed by doubt. "Perhaps," she murmured, wishing for this once that events could pattern the longing of the heart.

Danny squared his shoulders. "I don't care what happens to me. Blue Lightning must be returned to Captain Mallow, and Rufus must have the reward to bring back to this household."

"When will you go, Danny?" Jennet asked.

"Within the hour, eh Rufus?"

Rufus nodded, his face shining as he thought of the weight of the sack with a hundred dollars in it. Would they be gold or silver, he wondered. No matter. Their value would be the same. Melody, watching them and realizing that they would be leaving soon, got up to pack some food for their journey. She went deftly about her task, cutting slabs of journey-cake that was half meal and half berries, wrapping a generous slice from the cheese, polishing apples for them to put in their pockets.

"You'll be safe enough once you are out of this township," Jennet said. "Here, where there's been so much trouble, Danny could be apprehended; and you, Rufus, could be seized for being an accomplice."

"If we go through the woods to the turnpike, we'll avoid most of the houses; then we'll turn east at the crossroads."

"Deacon Phillips is the only one who might have an eye to you," Benoni said.

As they left the house, Melody stood on the doorstone. Rufus and Benoni went ahead to get the horses ready; Jennet followed them to the barn. Benoni would need her help this morning if the chores were ever to be done with Rufus away.

Danny put his hands on Melody's shoulders. The few words he had taught her could be said briefly and without need of her slate. "I'll come back," he said, shaping the words with his lips and putting her hand on his throat so that she could feel them. He held up three fingers, and she nodded; then all his fingers, and she nodded reluctantly. He opened and closed his hands several times.

Melody's eyes filled with tears as she thought of the space of time that might roll between them. She raised her hands and pointed to the woods; then she cupped her hands and made the sound of the cuckoo.

"I'll come to you at the lake, as you came to me," Danny said, "but I'll be an honest man then instead of a fugitive."

She shook her head, for when he lapsed into many words she had no way of knowing what he was saying.

Suddenly he took her hand in his and pressed it to his lips. "Love of my heart," he murmured; then he released her hand as quickly as he had taken it and stepped away to fill his eyes with the sight of her as she stood on the doorstone.

Rufus was calling from the barnyard where he stood with Willow and Blue Lightning saddled and bridled. Danny left Melody to join him. The two young men mounted their horses and rode off across the fields and into the shelter of the woods. Melody leaned against the doorpost and watched them go. Once before she had seen Danny leave, and she had felt as if something of herself was going with him.

"Dan," she called and waved. She kept on waving until they were out of sight. Thoughts beat and pressed within her, but they did not cause her anguish. She had taken a few steps along a wider road with Danny; she would wait for him until they could go the rest of the way together.

She turned her head quickly and saw Deacon Phillips standing near her.

"Your father?" he asked.

She shook her head.

"Your mother?" he said with raised voice.

She shook her head.

"Your brothers?" he shouted at her.

She shook her head and pointed behind her to the empty house.

Deacon Phillips turned and went back to his horse. He would return when someone was there with whom he could talk.

Chapter Eleven

Rufus and Danny rode off on Willow and Blue Lightning into a raw east wind with the heavy ground squelching under hoofs. The horses were eager and ready to put their strength into the road before them, but the boys restrained them. Blue's leg had healed well, but Danny wanted to return him in a fresh condition, and Willow could not be ridden hard because of the foal she was carrying.

They followed the road through the woods. When they crossed the lane that led up to the lake, Danny looked wistfully at it. The lake, hidden so deep in the woods, had been both his refuge and his salvation. How could he have known, he asked himself, when he first found it on that August night, that its mirror-smooth waters would be the witness of his first meeting with Melody.

The traveling was better when they reached the turnpike, for the road had a harder surface. They trotted for a mile or two, then dropped down to a walk. So much was there to talk about that they cared little whether they ran the horses or not, and Rufus said they would easily do the distance in two days, though it had taken Danny longer. Danny found stirring deep within him a love of the land he had come to. He had already given his heart to its people, as known in the Austins; but it was the land now that he saw with eyes of new feeling.

Everything had been against him at first; now everything seemed to be working with him.

Rufus told him stories he had heard from his father of the changes the land had seen in the rolling of a century. Footpaths had become roads, and crude cabins had given way to farmhouses; where once only forest had stood, now there were cleared fields and meadows. Churches and schools had come first in the long slow move toward civilization, then grist and lumber mills, stores, and inns. Once everyone had ridden saddle or pillion; now there were wagons and wheel carriages so that a whole family could ride over the road with only one horse to draw them.

"Even with your hard times, which I'm thinking were no more than a man pitting his strength against nature," Danny remarked, "you've had more of the good things of life than I've ever known."

"But you never had the wolves to disturb the flocks and trouble the herds! Why, Danny, time was when the horned cattle had to flee for their lives, and when the lambs who were put out to graze in the spring had to be rubbed with brimstone, gunpowder, and grease to keep the foxes from carrying them away!"

"Aye, but what you saved you had for your own, to put in your belly or your pocket," Danny reminded him. "With us, all but the least of our crop was marked for others. Indeed, we might be starving, but ships still left our docks loaded with produce for Liverpool and London. So little we had that it got to be a saying with us that if the next crop failed it would be the end of the world."

"For Ireland?"

"For us, the tenant farmers. No, the rich were well fed. Oh, there's no lovelier sight in the world than the potato patches in bloom, but there's none crueler a week later when the land is laid waste by blight and the smell of rotten vegetation is heavy on the air. There's panic and terror then among the people, and sadness and shame when a good green land cannot feed those who work it."

Rufus had often been hungry, but he had never known famine. "Was it that way before you left?"

Danny nodded and a look of sorrow came over his face. "During the summer that was my last in the old country, storm and east wind withered the potato patches, drought stunted the pastures, and cattle had to be killed. Then rain came so steadily that nothing could ripen, only rot. There were no crops to load in the carts to carry to market, and with no crops there was little joy on our faces or reason for thanksgiving in our hearts. Yet it was not food we wanted so much as to be master of a patch of soil–"

"A patch of soil?" Rufus repeated the phrase unbelievingly.

"Aye, that was all; and if not for a lifetime, then for the growing season."

"I'd not be content with so little," Rufus said.

"Would you want the world for yourself then?"

"No, not the world, but what I do want is a tract of my own, a hundred and sixty acres of land–meadow, arable, and forest, with a clear spring and a sheltered spot for a home, game in the woods, and no foxes, snakes, or crows to plague me. I'll have it soon too, in Ohio or Illinois, or even farther, in the new territory of Kansas."

Danny stared at his companion. "You wouldn't leave this countryside!"

"Indeed I would, and I shall as soon as I have the hundred dollars for my ox and wagon and the payment on the land."

"A hundred dollars!" Danny exclaimed. "That's what you will have tomorrow."

"And I'll know what to do with it."

"So we all hear tales of a green land," Danny said with a sigh. "For you it's beyond the rim of the hills; with me it was beyond the rim of the sea."

"Every man wants a piece of land he can call his own, where he can be his own master," Rufus said.

They rode along in silence for a while; then Danny commented, "A man can't be much of a master unless he has a woman in his house."

Rufus nodded.

They fell to talking about women, but Rufus, though he admitted freely that he would need one if the new life was to be well lived, said nothing to Danny about Martha Dunklee. And Danny, though he felt his heart aching for Melody the farther away he got from her, could not bring himself to speak of her to Rufus. He knew he had nothing but his heart to give her and that even in this free land a man must have more to offer than that.

When darkness began to come down, they found a farmer who agreed to give them food and shelter if they would split and stack two cords of wood for him the next morning. That delayed their leaving, but when the work that paid for their night was done, they were on the road again. The sun had not crossed the meridian and they had already gone more than half of their distance.

They spoke less, for as they neared the seacoast the countryside was strange to Rufus and he was busy exploring it with his eyes. Danny was busy trying to trace the route he had come in his wild dash to freedom more than three weeks ago. He recognized a house here and then a field; he remembered crossing a bridge; but the sure evidence was in the way Blue Lightning pricked up his ears and started to caper over the road. The more Danny held him in, the more excitedly he capered.

Then Danny saw the field where he had slept during the days he was working in the mill. Beyond the field, he knew, was a handsome white house where Captain Mallow lived and a large barn where Blue had once been stalled.

It was late afternoon when they tied their horses to the hitching posts and went up the steps of the white house.

Danny's heart sank within him as Rufus raised the heavy brass knocker and the sound it gave forth echoed against the silence. At that moment the immediate past slipped away from Danny, the past wherein he had known such kindness, and the future loomed before him full of uncertainty.

He did not doubt that he would receive justice; but he dared not hope that he would receive kindness comparable to that he had known in the Austin home. Perhaps he had had his share of kindness for a lifetime. If so, he would do his best to hold to the memory of it. He thought of Melody, and in that moment of waiting for the door to open, she seemed to be standing beside him, her hands held out, half open in her characteristic gesture. So often she could not give, so often she could only open her hands to receive what life would give to her, whether she understood or desired it.

The door was opened by a tall, well-built man with graying hair. The expression on his face was austere, but there was something about his keen blue eyes that said he had not lost the secret of laughter.

"I would speak with Captain Isaac Mallow," Rufus said. "I bear tidings of interest to him."

"Speak then," the captain answered gruffly.

"Sir, I have the honor of returning to you your stallion, Blue Lightning."

Captain Mallow's face had been stern, but at the name of his horse it lighted up with uncontrolled joy. "So," he said, breathing deeply, "he has been found at last!"

Rufus stepped aside and the captain came out of the house. He stood on the doorstep and looked at the two horses tied to the hitching posts. One was a heavy brown, the other a black of lighter build.

Captain Mallow turned on Rufus quickly. "This is the third time someone has tried to fool me!" he exclaimed angrily. "Now I wish I'd never allowed the Hue and Cry to post a reward. It's making people more dishonest than they are by nature." He faced about and went into the house.

"I beg you, sir, to look more closely," Rufus implored. "The present color of your horse is no more than a pot of dye my father gave him for safety."

Rufus knew that once Captain Mallow went into his house and shut the door behind him he would not open it again though they might thunder on it with their fists. His mother in mixing the dye, his father in applying it, had done their work too well. If Captain Mallow could not be persuaded to examine the horse, he and Danny would have to return as they had come and without the reward on which his heart was set.

"Sir, place your hands on him."

Yielding to Rufus's persuasion, Captain Mallow turned and looked again at the horses, but he kept on shaking his head. His glance was not wasted on Willow; it dwelt on the black stallion. The cropped tail and mane said no more to him than the sheenless color, but there was something about the bone and build of the animal that held him.

"The black is well bred," he admitted.

"Speak his name, sir, for he would know your voice though he's not heard it this month."

"I had not the training of him, so my voice would not call to him, and my man is not here today." Captain Mallow paused. "But there is something about the black, something familiar." He started down the steps of the house toward the horses.

Danny sprang forward and laid his hand on the captain's arm. "I swear the black one is yours, sir."

"Who are you to tell me what I alone know?"

"Who am I? Indeed, and I'm the very one to tell you for it was I who stole the horse and rode him through a dozen townships before I reached the shelter of Jared Austin's land."

"But who are you?" the captain asked, his curiosity aroused as much by the lilt in Danny's voice as by the earnest in his eyes.

"I'm Danny O'Dare of County Donegal in Ireland, but please God I'll soon be Danny O'Dare of New Hampshire."

Captain Mallow stood by the black stallion, placing his hands on withers and flanks, running them down strong legs. Blue nickered and tossed his head.

The captain began to smile. "It might be–" he muttered to himself. Turning to Rufus he said, "This horse does indeed bear a likeness to my stallion."

Rufus flashed a smile. "I knew you'd know him, sir, once you got your hands on him."

"Aye, but does he know me?"

"Sir," Danny said, "is the stallion's stall unoccupied?"

"Every stall is empty. The horses have not yet come in from pasture."

"Then let us lead Blue Lightning to the barn and let him find his own stall."

Captain Mallow nodded in agreement. There was reasonableness in the request, a reasonableness which he could not deny. Lover of horses as he was and cognizant of their ways, he knew that the horse had often settled a question which had baffled the owner.

"Very well," he said. "Bring the horse to the barn." Turning, he led the way across the yard and through the gathering twilight.

Danny untied Blue Lightning. Walking on one side of him, with Rufus on the other, they followed the captain to the barn.

"Will he remember?" Rufus whispered anxiously. "It's been near a month since he last saw his own stall."

"I've never known a horse to forget the one place in the world he can call his own," Danny replied.

The captain was waiting for them at the entrance to the barn. Danny slipped the bridle off Blue Lightning and slapped him gently on the rump. The horse stepped forward hesitantly into the space that was filled with the dusk of oncoming night and sweet with the smell of hay.

"Which stall did he call his?" Danny asked.

"The sixth on the left," the captain answered. "It's the best one, and I've always kept it for my stallion. It's had no occupant this past month."

Slowly Blue Lightning walked down the wooden floor, lifting his head and whinnying questioningly, then imperatively, as if to demand an answer from the mares that should have been there. He stopped after he had gone a few paces and stamped on the floor, then pawed impatiently. Seven stalls there were on each side; all deep in straw; all empty. Fourteen mangers were filled with hay for the horses when they came in from pasture and for the one whose return had been long awaited.

Blue Lightning walked past two stalls, then turned in to the third on the right; but before all four feet were in the straw he backed out again and deliberately crossed to the stalls on the other side. He paused again and tossed his head; then he walked on almost to the end of the line. At the sixth stall on the left he turned and walked in. A tremulous whinny echoed in the silence of the barn as the horse went toward the manger and started eating.

Danny looked at Rufus. "You can always trust a horse."

Rufus let out a sigh. He had not realized until that moment that he had been holding his breath.

"Well, I'll–" the captain began, as confirmation of his hope took words away from him. "Well, I'll–" he began again, but delight rendered him speechless.

Danny followed Blue into his stall. He put his arms around the horse and rubbed his cheek against the horse's neck. "It's thanking you I am," he whispered into Blue's ear.

Danny undid the buckles on the girth and took the saddle off. The stallion's back was damp under the saddle and some of the dye had come away. The inside of the saddle was stained, and where it had rested a faint dappling that was Blue Lightning's natural color could be seen.

Captain Mallow stood beside his horse and put his arm around his neck, resting his head against the velvet nose; then he went to the grain bin to get a measure of oats. After he had fed the horse, he turned to Rufus and Danny.

"Come, boys, into the house with me. You must be hungry after your journey; and while we eat our dinner, you shall tell me how the stallion came into your hands."

"It's a story worth telling, sir," Rufus said.

"I'll warrant it is, and when it's done there's a reward awaiting." His eyes twinkled as he looked from Rufus to Danny. "Even divided between you, it will give each one of you a sizable sum."

"But none of it is for me," Danny began. "You see, I–"

Rufus motioned him to silence as they followed the captain out of the barn and into the house.

Captain Mallow was so pleased with the return of Blue Lightning that during dinner he could talk of nothing else. Rufus tried more than once to tell how it was that the horse had come to be in the Austin barn, but Captain Mallow kept interrupting him.

"Your story can wait, my lad, for now that I have my horse again, there are things I would tell you about him."

"And the reward, sir?"

The captain laughed heartily. "The gold has been in this house more than a month, and it will lose none of its glitter if it waits an hour longer before it passes from my hand to yours."

Danny sighed with relief. He was in no haste to tell his part of the story.

A noble meal it was that Captain Mallow's servant produced for them and one worthy of the celebration fitting the return of a valued horse. There was a roast goose dripping with fat, potatoes each one as large as a man's hand, greens from the garden, and for dessert, a pudding that made Danny roll his eyes and Rufus smack his lips. The captain beamed at his two guests and cared little whether he ate himself, so long as he could heap their plates with food and fill their ears with tales of Blue Lightning.

The stallion had been sired in Africa and brought to America when he was a colt. "I was master of the vessel that bore him," the captain said. "Many a treasure had we carried in our hold on past voyages, but never a one like that yearling. He was marked by beauty from the time he was foaled, with his small pricked ears, sensitive muzzle, and wide flaring nostrils. And intelligence was his from his first breath."

"Indeed so," Danny agreed. "Beauty and intelligence have developed well, for he's got them both now that he has his full size."

"He's lively of temperament and strong of sinew," Captain Mallow went on, "and he's as sound in character as he is in wind. Aye, I love him the way I loved the ships I've sailed, and I've hopes for a line of progeny from him that will be second to none."

Rufus's eyes grew wide at the thought of what they had sheltered in their barn.

"It's the Barb blood in him that has given him what he has." The captain sighed. Endless as the stallion's fine points were, he was near the end of extolling them.

"It is," Danny nodded, "for a drop of blood is worth an inch of bone."

Captain Mallow looked at him shrewdly. "You know about horses, then?"

"Arra, but I fell from my cradle on to the back of one of them!"

The captain leaned closer. "It's an odd twist of the tongue you have, my lad."

"It's from Ireland I am, sir, as I have told you, and not long in this land either."

"From Ireland!" he exclaimed. Then a light broke over his face. "But 'twas an Irish lad who made off with the stallion. Can you tell me anything about him?"

"Sure and I've been telling you since I first stood on your doorstep that I'm the lad."

"You!"

"And my friend here is the one who apprehended me; so he must receive the reward."

"I thought you both apprehended the stallion and brought him here."

Danny shook his head.

Rufus tried to explain to Captain Mallow what had happened, telling the story briefly as he had heard it from Danny and then as he had seen it furthering itself during the last few days.

"You look too good a boy to be a horse thief" was the captain's only comment as he left the table and came back with a bag. He opened it and counted out a hundred dollars in gold coin, dividing it into two piles. "I'd thought you'd each have a share, but if I rightly understand what happened, the whole must go to Rufus Austin." He pushed the two piles across the table to Rufus.

"Thank you, sir," Rufus said as he pocketed the money carefully.

Captain Mallow kept his eyes on Rufus. Finally, as Rufus made no move, he said to him, "What are you waiting for?"

"I–I don't know."

"Nor do I. Go along now. You've done your work. You've earned your reward. I'll take care of your friend."

"But, Captain Mallow–"

The captain waved his hand. "Daniel O'Dare can stay here tonight. Tomorrow will be soon enough to hand him over to the sheriff. That's his reward, isn't it, boy?"

"Yes sir, and I'm ready and willing to accept it." Danny turned to Rufus and grasped his hand. "You must go, Rufus," he said. "We both have our rights and I'm content." He walked to the door with Rufus and went down the steps to watch him ride off.

When Danny entered the room again, Captain Mallow called to him to come back to the table where he was still sitting, the empty money bag before him.

"Why did you do it, boy? Why did you let evil take your hand?"

Danny shook his head. Thinking back to that night when he and Blue Lightning had cantered around the pasture, then over the stone wall and away down the road, he could find no easy words of explanation. "A bit of bitterness, sir," he said quietly, "a bit of skylarking."

The captain looked at him in a fatherly way. "There's only one thing to do, you know, and that is to turn you over to the law."

Danny squared his shoulders. "I know."

"In the morning—"

"Sir," Danny said, as fear of what might happen crept into him, "I didn't mean to do what I did, and I brought your horse back of my own free will."

"I know that, boy, and I wish I knew a way to save you from the consequences of your act, for you seem a good lad and you've a fine feeling for horses."

"I'd work the skin off my hands for you," Danny promised.

"That's not the point. It's the money. The Hue and Cry Society of Portsmouth put up the money that's been paid over to Rufus Austin. They're entitled to have you as the apprehended thief, or else they must have their money paid back to them."

Danny hung his head. "I don't want to be known as a thief," he said earnestly. "I want my name to be as good in this land as my father's is in Ireland."

"Aye, there's the rub," Captain Mallow said meditatively. "Satisfy the law and keep your name unsmirched. I know of no way you could do it unless you put up the money yourself."

"Oh!" Danny exclaimed. "But if I go to work in the mill and work hard till I earn a hundred dollars, will that not do it, sir?"

Captain Mallow thought for a moment. "The procedure is unusual and will take all my wits to explain what is going on; but if you can make restitution for the reward, we can keep you from the law."

"I'll sleep in a field, I'll eat the least I can to keep body and soul together, I'll–"

"If you like hay, you can sleep in my barn; and you can have one meal a day if you'll help exercise the horses after your time in the mill."

"Like hay!" Danny exclaimed. "Why, sir, I'd scarce exchange the kiss of a maiden for the tickling of hay on my cheek."

"You're not made for a mill, my lad, but such work is the only kind I know where you can make ready money these days." The captain counted with his fingers on the table. "It might take you until the spring."

"The clacking of wheels and the reek of looms are not like the sound of hoofs or the smell of a horse, but they'll be worth enduring if at the end of the time I can know myself as a free man and honest."

The captain wagged a finger at him. "It's not for yourself alone you want to be called an honest man."

"My thousand sorrows!" Danny exclaimed, drawing his hand over his face as if to take away what was telltale.

"For yourself you wouldn't care. You'd go elsewhere where your name was not known," Captain Mallow said with a twinkle in his keen blue eyes. "Aye, Danny boy, I've not seen the way of a man with a maid for nothing! It's because there's someone you'll soon give your name to that you want it to be unsullied."

The color mounted slowly in Danny's cheeks.

"Is she beautiful, lad?"

Danny nodded.

"Does she praise God?"

Danny nodded.

"And the horses?"

"She's got a way with all creatures," Danny said quietly, "as if she understood them better than men."

"And she's got your heart in her hands!"

"Not to her knowing, sir."

The captain inclined his head. "Women folk have a way of knowing sooner than we do. You're young, Danny O'Dare, and you've a long life before you, and a good life too, but you can thank God that you met a lass who held a standard even before you knew you loved her and has kept you to it. I'm an old man, but I hope I'll live to see your hands joined in service and in worship. Come now, and I'll show you where you can sleep."

"Sir," Danny said as he got up from the table, "I've naught but the clothes on my back and they belong to Rufus Austin, but is it a pen you'll be having and a bit of paper I could write on?"

"You shall have them," the captain said with a smile.

"It's a letter I must write," Danny said. "She thought I would be back in three days, and now three seasons will roll around before I can take her hand in mine."

Danny wrote his letter and then they went to the barn. He mounted the ladder to the hayloft. There was a crack in the wooden wall through which he could watch the captain go back to the house. Danny slipped down the ladder and groped his way to Blue Lightning's stall. In the darkness he put his hands on him, then around his neck.

"Oh, Blue," he whispered, "if it hadn't been for you, such a wealth of goodness would never be mine. Whisht, but I've more to tell you than can be said now. I must be up tomorrow at the sparrow's chirp to find work in the mill, but I'll tell you more a night from now."

He mounted the ladder again. Two other workmen of the captain's slept in the loft, but it was late and they were deep in slumber. Unobserved and safe, Danny knelt in the darkness with the hay prickling his legs and the fragrance around him and the munching of the horses down below. He might have been a boy at his mother's knee, so easy it was to pray, and a few moments later, to close his eyes in sleep.

Chapter Twelve

A full moon rose high in the sky as Rufus rode on his way, the heavy coins in his leather pouch jingling in accompaniment to the sound of Willow's hoofs. Near midnight he spied a fern brake by a stream and stopped there to rest. Tethering Willow, he made a bed for himself in the ferns and did not wake until the moon had given way to the sun and the horse was whinnying for attention.

"Heigh-ho, my lass, you've a hollow place in you as I have, but we'll hope to fill them both at the first farm we come to."

Rufus washed in the stream and drank deeply of the flowing water; then he led Willow to the stream. She bent her long neck and plunged her heavy head in, not drinking so much as playing with the water, pushing her nose up and down in it, blowing out through her nostrils, shaking her head, and pawing at pebbles in early morning frolicsomeness.

Rufus watched her, smiling to himself. She was an old horse and almost all of her twelve years had been spent with the Austins. Rufus could scarcely remember any horse before Willow. He would miss her when he went West. He ran his hand over her strong body and with a sudden pang realized that he would not be there to see her colt in the spring. But go he must, for the West called to him and the wherewithal was now in his hands. Once he had wished he could ride

Willow to the new territory, but he knew that would not do. He needed a young horse, a strong stallion; a brood mare as old as Willow would only be a care. And now it was Martha Dunklee who filled his thoughts. He had not yet asked her for her hand, in so many words, but he knew her well enough to know that when he did she would not refuse him.

He tightened the saddle girth, slipped the bridle over Willow's head, and mounted. Willow, her playfulness put behind her, stepped briskly along the road with her rider singing aloud to the morning. The road had many a bend and there were no houses to be seen, but it was not long before the smell of wood smoke pervaded the air.

A small, well-set frame house came into view. Rufus rode up to its door. The woman who answered his knock did not see him as a stranger, but as one who needed refreshment. She held the door wide open to him while the rest of the family, gathered for the morning meal, instantly made a place for him at the table. As a plate was filled for Rufus, the oldest boy slipped out to the barn to get a measure of oats for Rufus's horse.

Rufus paid well for his food with the news he brought and the tales he told. When the man of the house said he could do with a strong pair of arms that day to help in threshing some grain, Rufus stayed on, and Willow was turned out to pasture.

It was not until the afternoon of the fifth day since his departure that Rufus trotted down the road and saw his home in sight. Three miles back, Willow had pricked up her ears and begun lifting her feet springily as if she were traveling on moss. With no urging, she had broken into a trot, and Rufus had let her suit her pace to her desire on the last stretch.

Rufus was glad he was nearing home. He was impatient to get into the stride of his new life, to talk with his father and mother, to see Martha Dunklee. He was tired of being alone with only Willow to talk to, and the gold coins weighed on his mind as they did in his leather pouch. He would be glad to put the treasure in a safe place for a while.

He could see Melody sitting on the doorstone as he drew near. Her blue dress made a bright patch of color; her brown hair falling forward hid her face as she played with a pair of kittens in her lap. He wanted to shout, so glad was he to see her, but the sound of her name stuck in his mouth, and he swallowed hard against the bitter taste left by the realization that no matter how loudly he called, she would not hear. Had she been lying on the ground with one ear pressed to the earth, she would have caught the sound of his coming from a distance and been ready to greet him, but it was not until he had put Willow in the barn and come across the yard to stand before her that she was aware of his presence.

With one of those curiously muffled cries, she put the kittens on the ground and stood up quickly, flinging her arms around Rufus and nestling her head against him, burrowing into the warmth of his presence; then she stood away from him and Rufus could see by the urgency on her face that there was something she wanted to tell him. He looked for the slate that was her constant possession. Not seeing it on the ground beside her or propped against the doorstone, he could only assume that she had been alone all day and had found no reason to carry it.

Her swift gestures implied that no one else was home, but where the rest of the family had gone or why seemed beyond her power to convey. That their being away had something to do with the Dunklee family was all that Rufus could make out. He felt then that he would gladly have given one of his gold coins to have Danny with them, for Danny would have divined what Melody was trying to say.

Hopelessly aware of her inadequacy, Melody put her head in her hands, sat down on the doorstone, and started to cry. Rufus knelt beside her, trying to comfort her, but his inadequacy was as frightening as hers. No sound accompanied her sorrow; gently heaving shoulders and slowly coursing tears marked a grief that could no longer be contained.

Rufus left her to herself and went into the house. Unbuckling the leather pouch from his belt, he tossed it on the table; but the contents might have been lead for the pleasure they brought him then. He sighed. Money was value and should be put in safekeeping until its use could be determined. However weary he was of it, he would safeguard it until his father's return.

He opened the fireplace cupboard to stow the pouch in it. There were his mother's precious herbal and his father's bundle of accounts. The Bible was there and beside it stood another book. Rufus took the book out to make room for the gold coins.

"Mr. Whittier's poems!" he exclaimed, surprised at finding something beside the Bible. He had not known their household possessed another book, for always the Bible had been their storehouse and they had drawn from it for diversion as well as improvement.

The poems opened where a marker was and the marker fell to the floor. Rufus bent over to pick up the piece of paper. Four words on it caught his eye and held his attention–

SCHOOL FOR THE DEAF

The words took their own shape in his mind, reminding him of what Jared had said about the school, and he found himself saying over and over, "Hope for my sister; hope for my sister." A quietness came over him that was something new and rare. To it, his inner ear was opened.

There was a faint whispering sound from the back log on the hearth, but Rufus did not hear it. A light wind tapped a branch against the window, but Rufus did not hear it. The clock ticked time on, but he did not hear it either. Rufus put the slip of paper back in the book and set the book away in the cupboard, in front of the leather pouch. A smile wove itself across his powerful face.

A few moments later Rufus caught the sound of hoofs and of wheels turning. He went quickly to the door. It was Pepper, hitched to the four-seated wagon. His father and mother sat on the front seat in their Sunday clothes. Benoni, dressed equally well, was just getting out of the wagon to hold Pepper's head. Rufus went past Melody on the doorstone, calm now and with dry eyes.

"Who was it?" he asked, standing beside his parents, for their manner and clothes proclaimed their errand.

"John Dunklee," Jared answered. "They wanted to keep him until you got back, but none of us knew when that might be. It was better so. Sorrow plows a deep enough furrow without prolonging it."

"He was a good man."

"My first friend in these parts," Jared went on, "and the one who always stood by me. His life was full and blessed, but it's never easy to lose a friend."

"Melody tried to tell me, but I couldn't understand her."

"Melody knows little about death." Jared sighed, realizing how much more there was that the girl must learn some day.

Jennet got down from the wagon and stood beside Pepper, stroking him. "Such worthy words they put on his stone," she murmured, "and they say that Silvanus Sumner stayed up all last night cutting them so that the stone might be erected today. Such worthy words!

> He folded not his hands in life
> But worked for good of all—

I can't remember all the lines, there were so many." She put her hands to her eyes; then she left, taking brisk steps into the house.

Jared watched her go. "Her heart's been torn this afternoon, but she'll feel better when she gets the dinner cooking."

"How was Martha?"

"Brave as a Dunklee would be," Jared replied; then he shook his head, thinking of John Dunklee's daughter. "Young Martha will have no life of her own until her brothers are grown. It's her strong shoulders that must help her mother bear the burden of the farm."

Rufus dropped his gaze quickly. He did not want even his father to know what was in his heart.

That night, after they had eaten well and heavy hearts had grown lighter, Rufus told them of his journey and of what Danny had chosen to do. When he came to the end of his story, he went to the cupboard and took out the leather pouch. He placed it on the table. No one said anything. Benoni was the first to lean forward and touch it; the feel of the hard round coins confirmed in his mind what the clinking sound had suggested.

"The reward?" he asked eagerly.

Rufus nodded.

"A hundred dollars!"

Jennet's hand went to her mouth to stifle a cry. Better than anyone else, she knew what a hundred dollars meant to Rufus. To lose their neighbor and her eldest son in one day was more than even her stout heart could bear.

Melody looked from her mother to her brothers–Benoni's face was eager, Rufus's was impassive. She was puzzled. She turned to her father, trying to understand what was going on. Jared's face was calm. He looked tired, and the tiredness gave him years, but there was peace in his face which gave Melody a haven for her questioning. He would tell her in time what was taking place. She would be patient. She folded her hands together.

"So now you are leaving us?" The quietness of inevitability was in Jared's words.

Rufus shook his head.

"Then what are you going to do with so much money?"

"It's for Melody," Rufus said; "so she may be educated according to her particular need, if you and mother are willing."

Jared looked at Jennet. She opened her mouth to speak, but no words came. She nodded her head slowly. The impulse of acquiescence came not from her so much as through her.

Jared looked across the table at his son. All that he wanted to say was locked within him as Melody's words were locked within her. He got up from the bench and went around to stand beside Rufus. He put both hands on his shoulders and looked into the face of his eldest son. "God will bless you," he said.

Rufus bowed his head and murmured, "Thank you." He realized then that what meant most of all to him was his father's approval; now he had secured it.

Rufus turned away quickly and left the room. Benoni saw him cross the yard to the barn and followed him. Whatever Rufus was going to do in the barn, he wanted to help him.

Jennet looked at Jared and reached out to take hold of his hand. "How is it possible," she asked, "for the same heart to break with sorrow and then with joy all in the same day?"

"I don't know," he said, smiling at her. "But that such things can happen is part of the greatness of life."

Melody had been watching them. When she saw them smile, she knew that something good had happened, something about which her father would tell her in time.

Later that night as they sat on the settle together, Jared showed Melody the slip of paper that described the school in Hartford. He told her as best he could what was ahead of her for the coming year; then he wrote on her slate, "Rufus has made this possible, but Danny has had something to do with it." He shaped a circle with thumb and forefinger. As she watched him, he opened the circle gradually. It was their sign that she would understand more in good time.

She nodded, pleased. She took the chalk from him and wrote, "I love Danny O'Dare."

Jared gazed at her untroubled blue eyes that had such depths, the same depths which her mind must have and which now stood some chance of being sounded. He wondered what she knew of love–she who fondled animals, played games with her brothers, and showed her affection in tender ways with Jennet and himself.

"Love?" He said the word aloud and she reached forward to put her hand on his throat to feel the sound of it. He repeated the word as he had seen Danny do when she placed her fingers on his throat. After a moment he wrote on the slate, "What is it like to you?"

She smiled mischievously and took the chalk. She wiped the slate clean and drew an outline of hills with the sun peeping over their rim; then she drew another few lines, and another, to indicate that the sun was rising. With a throaty little sound that was almost like a laugh, she wiped the slate and drew the sun shining in full and risen splendor.

Jared nodded, knowing what she meant. It was like that to her–simple, clear, shining; coming gradually, then shedding its fullness on her life.

She wiped away the sun and wrote, "Love is stronger than death."

Jared gazed at her. So she knew about those two ends of the pole and the link love made between them. He drew her to him and kissed her; then Melody, happy and satisfied, wriggled away from his embrace and went off to help her mother.

Jared sat looking into the fire; yet it was not the flames licking around the log he saw or the soot-blackened bricks behind them; it was a slender slate stone marking the grave of a good man and on the stone the words:

> *Oh, happy place, we all must say,*
> *Where all but love is done away.*

Chapter Thirteen

It was a long winter, and a lonely one for two people especially–Melody Austin in Hartford, Connecticut, and Danny O'Dare in Portsmouth, New Hampshire. But the loneliness was an incentive to work, and the Austin hearth was where their thoughts turned and found a meeting place.

Rufus had with good grace given up all thoughts of asking Martha Dunklee to be his bride for a year at least, while she helped her mother with the farm. No Conestoga wagons rolled by their door during the winter months to tempt him with their sails, but deep within his heart Rufus cherished his dream, and in an old dye pot he had begged from his mother he began a collection of small coins.

At the rate the coins accumulated, it would take years to get his needed sum, but Rufus had been deeply moved at the way the money had come for Melody's schooling. Slowly he was acquiring some of the patient trustfulness that marked his father. He threw his strong frame into the work of the farm, releasing Jared for more of his chosen work and Benoni for his, and when Jared came home with a pocket of coins, he never failed to drop one or two into the dye pot for Rufus.

Benoni went to school and in his free time painted furniture. He would often go miles to a distant house for a chair or a clock which he carried home in his arms or strapped to his horse. The conventional designs of overflowing bowls of fruit or clusters of flowers were generally the choice of his customers, and Benoni worked over them carefully, using the costly metallic powders with sparing hands. Gold and bronze would hold their luster indefinitely, and Benoni thought proudly that long after he was gone, mute pieces of furniture would speak his skill as walls once drab spoke his father's.

The work that Jared could find was lessening with the years. Unwillingly at first and then of necessity, Jared admitted that the machine was taking a hold on man which could not be denied. At first he and many others thought that machines would have their day, and then men would slip back to the satisfactions of handwork; but with each passing year the machines made greater inroads.

Walls were being covered with wallpaper–and not from Paris or London, but from nearby Boston: available to any who could afford improvement in their homes. Yards of cheap materials were pouring from the mills, materials which people made into garments and curtains and bedcovers. Many of the countrywomen still wove their materials as Jennet did, but the end was in sight for home weaving.

"People don't want things beautiful any more; they want them quickly," Jared commented one night.

"And cheap," Benoni added.

Jared deplored the decline of handcrafts, but there were few voices raised with his. Most of the voices were raised in praise of the new ways.

"When all the work is done by machines," Benoni said one night as they sat by the fire, "people won't know what to do with their time."

"They'll never invent a machine to knead bread," Jennet replied in defense of one of her crafts.

"No, nor one to hoe corn," Jared added.

Rufus looked up with a twinkle in his eye. "Nor one to put horses out of the running."

There were days when the snow piled silently around the house and the wind blew it into deep drifts. All they could do was shovel a path to the barn so that the animals would be cared for, then spend the rest of the time by the hearth. If a letter from Danny or Melody had come before then, the reading and rereading gave them plenty to talk about.

Danny was working hard in the mill and saving all that he earned, for the captain was giving him two meals now instead of one, and even clothes came his way and a pair of shoes to help him out. There was plenty of talk in his letters about Captain Mallow and his horses, but little talk about the mill itself.

"Poor lad," Jennet commented after one of his letters had been read. "He was born for the outside and anyone can see he's sick at heart with being inside so much." She shuddered, remembering it had not been so long ago that she had thought of a mill as a place for Melody.

Jared chuckled. "Here it's midwinter and the snow is three feet deep on the ground, but Danny wants to know when I'll be plowing! He tells me to be sure and give Willow brawn broth when she foals! I'll not plow until April, and the colt is not due until May."

"Ah, but that's where his heart is, and he's thinking ahead to the things he loves and understands to help him bear the hardness of the present. I only hope he won't sicken in body," Jennet added, "for I doubt if the captain would know how to care for him."

"God fits the back to the burden," Jared said, "and Danny has a strength in him which is not all muscle."

Melody's letters came each week and brought something of her presence into the household. From Jared to Benoni they missed her as they would the sun on a dreary day, but it was Jennet who missed her most of all. It was not because she was deprived of someone upon whom she could lavish care–drops of daisy oil or hot raisins in her ears; it was a need for her company, silent as it was.

"Oh, Jared, you don't think Danny will take her far away, do you?"

Jared shook his head. "Danny's found what he was seeking. I think it's here he will stay and put down his roots."

Melody's first letters were precise and dutiful, but gradually they expanded into more fullness of expression. She who once had to learn to steel herself against the attitude of others because she was different, now found herself in an environment where she was no different. The burden and bewilderment of living began to ease for her, and the comfort that came into her life was apparent in her letters.

The year had gone only half way when the head of the school wrote Jared to say that the work which often took two years to accomplish was being done by his daughter in one; that she was unusually responsive and when the doors of learning had begun to open a little for her, she had pushed them wide. Her fingers, more agile than many a child's, had taken to the manual alphabet, and she was even mastering a small range of sounds. Awkward as the sounds still might be when she returned home, if there was someone there with love enough and patience to continue the work, Melody might find that a degree of utterance would not be wholly denied her.

Jared and Jennet did not bemoan the fact that there was no hope given for her hearing. They had accepted that in the early years of her life. But as Melody acquired a means of communication, she was gaining more than they had ever dreamed for her. Barriers had separated Melody from the world, but the things she was learning–speech through her fingers and control of her voice–were overcoming the barriers. No longer was she a stranger in a strange land. She was one of a group of boys and girls who were working together in the endeavor to overcome their handicap.

Jennet, who had once seen Melody's affliction as a judgment on herself, now saw it as a rare challenge. Melody, in accepting the challenge, found new meaning in her life. The affliction might remain, but Melody would move forward into life little different from her fellows. Alertness was hers, and the capacity to think long and peacefully, since the world could not intrude its clamor on her quiet.

One day a letter came to the Austin household, and in it Danny told them that his earnings for the past four months had all gone to the sum that was slowly accumulating and which Captain Mallow would pay over to the Hue and Cry. "Sure and I spent the money this week on myself, and a book it was I bought. Though what I do with it will be my present to Melody, and a secret it will be from her until I can give it myself."

Jared and Jennet read on eagerly. Danny had gone to a bookshop in town after his work in the mill and purchased a book that described the manual alphabet. "I keep it under the hay where I sleep and in the morning when the light comes I study it. At night when my work is done and the horses have been bedded, I study it if there's a lamp at hand. My fingers are clumsy still, and it's slow the words are in coming, but I'm thinking they'll gain willingness the way the horses do when they catch on to what it is you want of them.

"It's a long winter, the longest I've ever known, and it's lonely I am; for though I'm with good people, I'm far from those I love. But the sun will soon be growing stronger, and when it begins to melt the ridges on roads, there'll be more in view than the springtime."

"Bless the boy," Jennet said, as she went on with her spinning; and Jared tucked the letter away in the fireplace cupboard.

On a fine morning in early May, a young man came riding down the highway. The sheen on the coat of his chestnut mare matched the sheen on the leaves, and the gaiety of his manner matched that of the birds. He was singing, as they were, with his head thrown back and the wind rippling his shock of heavy black hair. The road was new to his horse but familiar to him; so he guided her over crossroads and at turnings.

When the afternoon shadows had begun to lengthen, he saw ahead of him a white house almost hidden by the lilacs that were growing beside it. He stopped his singing to breathe deeply of the fragrance that filled the air; then he reined his horse in to a walk and drew her over to the grassy border of the road so that his approach might be made without the warning sound of hoofbeats. At the hitching post he brought the mare to a halt and swung himself off the saddle. He fastened her and stroked her shining coat, whispering a few words of praise into her ears; then he went up to the door and raised his hand to knock.

Within, there had been the sound of voices as a family sat at table, but silence followed the knocking; then there could be heard the swift steps of a woman running across a bare floor, followed by a man's more even tread.

"The blessing of God be with you," Danny said as Jennet Austin opened the door to him.

Jennet let out a glad cry and flung her arms around Danny, clasping him to her as she would one of her own tall sons who had been away for too long.

When Jennet released him, Jared came forward and put his hand in Danny's. "It's good to see you, Danny O'Dare. We knew you'd be coming soon."

Rufus and Benoni came to the door and shook hands with the lad who had become like a brother to them, adding their welcome to that of their parents.

"You've grown!" Jennet exclaimed.

"And not only in height," Jared remarked as he saw how the lean frame had filled out.

Rufus and Benoni went to the hitching post to appraise the chestnut mare, and when they rejoined the group on the doorstone, they were loud in their approval.

"She's worth a pretty penny," Rufus said knowledgeably. "How did you get her when all your money went elsewhere?"

"Sure and I had to have a horse to put under my saddle!" Danny laughed, rolling his eyes in merriment.

"You bought her?"

"I didn't borrow or steal her, and that's my word with my life upon it."

"They'll give you no peace until you tell them," Jared said.

"It was Captain Mallow himself gave her to me," Danny explained. "Two days ago I brought him my earnings–all the weeks in the mill since I started that September day at three dollars a week. He counted it out and put it away to be given to the Society; then he took my hand in his and said, 'I'm proud to know an honest man.' That's what he said to me."

"But the horse?" Benoni begged.

"Aye, I'm coming to that," Danny said with another laugh. "The captain took me to the pasture where the two-year-olds were grazing, three of them sired by Blue Lightning, and their dams among the finest in the country. 'Choose the one you want, for it's yours to remember me by,' he said."

"Danny!" Rufus exclaimed admiringly.

"Was it hard to choose?" Benoni asked.

Danny shook his head. "All spring I'd been exercising them, and there was one I took to more than the others–I don't know why, for they were all quick to respond and strong in wind and limb."

"What do you call her?"

"Sure and I call her Cuckoo. That's not her name on the register, but it's what I've called her to myself ever since I started to ride her."

"A fair enough name," Jared commented, "and easy to call." He tried saying it. "It rolls off the tongue well."

"And what's nicer than the bird that calls in the long spring nights! Where's Melody?" Danny asked.

Jennet looked around and cast her eyes toward the barn, though she knew that if Melody were anywhere near, she would have joined them by now. "She must have gone to the woods," Jennet said. "Perhaps she's at the lake. She's gone there every evening since she got back from school the last week in April."

"I'll be going there after her."

Jennet put her arm through Danny's and started with him to the house. "Not until you've some food in your stomach," she said stoutly, "for I'll not have the hungry look come over your face while you're under our roof."

She made Danny sit down at the table and partake of the meal they had just finished, for plenty remained in the pot. While he ate, she told him of Melody: what the year at school had done for her, and how she had grown.

Jared joined them. "Rufus and Benoni are caring for your mare," he said, "and your saddle too. They're glad to have you back again. We knew we hadn't lost you, Danny, though we missed you sorely."

Danny pushed his empty plate away as he looked at Jennet and Jared. He wanted nothing between himself and them as he spoke the words that had lain in his heart for long and had grown wings during the past two days.

"It's Melody who has held my heart in her hands since first I've known her," he said earnestly, "and it's you I'm asking if I may speak with her."

Jennet said nothing, but her eyes filled with tears.

"It's been my prayer," Jared said quietly, "that with so much denied Melody in life she would find a good man's love. I have no doubt in my mind but that you are a good man, Danny, and that your love will fill the empty places in her life."

Danny nodded solemnly. He could not trust himself to speak.

"You have our consent to ask Melody for what is hers to give–her heart and her hand," Jared said. Then he smiled.

"But there'll be little asking needed, for they've been yours this long time."

Danny looked too happy to speak.

"We'll be glad to have you farm this land with us and live near at hand," Jared added, "for when Rufus goes West, there'll be no one to help with the land since Benoni wants to go journeying."

"Oh," Danny sighed, "but it's running over, my cup is!" He rose from the table. "I'm going to the lake where she's waiting for me."

Jared took the boy's outstretched hand and closed his two hands over it. "Only this word would I say to you, Danny O'Dare, but it has the long secret of true marriage behind it. Two are joined together to face life's joys and share its sorrows, but a time may come when one must be strong enough for two. Because of Melody being what she is, you may be the one. Should any hard thing happen in your life, as can happen in any life, can you be strong enough for two?"

There was silence within the house, but outside the air was throbbing with the singing of birds.

Danny spoke slowly, surely. "Yes, Jared Austin, I can be if I remember where my strength lies; and it is Melody who keeps taking me back to the Scriptures she likes so well to read. She will not let me forget."

They went to the door together; then Jared and Jennet stood there watching Danny as he walked across the fields and into the woods. There was a spring to his step like the lilt in his voice and the distance was soon put behind him. After he had gone from their view, they still went on watching. Jennet caught her breath in a half sob. Jared put his arm around her.

"It's a time for rejoicing," he chided gently.

"I know," she said. "I know, but sometimes there are tears when the heart is alive with joy."

Danny found the overgrown road and followed it. His heart was pounding within him, and though he was running now up the slope, his feet felt like lead and the distance seemed longer than the journey he had made across the Atlantic. The woods were full of song. Hermit thrushes were fluting to each other and the distant singing of wood thrushes sweetened the air. Nearing the opening in the trees, Danny paused to get his breath; then he approached slowly and saw the lake lying before him, its surface mirroring the perfection of the sky.

He halted. Leaning back against the smooth gray bark of a beech, he made the call of the cuckoo; then he brought his hands up over his head and clapped them sharply. The hollow sound echoed across the stillness. A few feet in front of him was the granite rock. If Melody were waiting, she would be there. It was not anything they had arranged, just something they knew.

Slowly a head appeared around the rock, a brown head with its thick hair caught neatly in a net. A pair of wide blue eyes stared at the lad leaning against the beech. A smile broke across a familiar face, and two hands came together in an answering clap.

Melody had been sitting with her head against the rock and her feet at the water's edge. Now she drew her feet under her and stood up, smoothing her dress as she rose. She leaned against the rock as Danny leaned against the beech and for a few moments neither one of them could move, nor did they want to.

What Danny saw was a girl grown tall and shapely with a full-fitting dress that fell almost to her ankles. Her face was marked by gentleness, and it was older than the face of the girl he had known, but it was serene and peaceful, as if some quiet mastery had come to her. She stood with the stillness of the lake behind her, and behind it the stillness of the forest. So like her life, Danny thought, much of it simple, clear, evident; much of it impenetrable yet holding beauty.

Melody saw a young man whose once-haunted face and shadowed eyes had given way to a direct gaze. The hollows in his cheeks had filled out. He no longer wore the pinched and frightened look. There was instead a look of power, of assurance. She saw him as a prisoner would see someone who had brought the key to freedom.

She opened her mouth. "Dan–ny." The sound was unmistakable.

"Melody," he said, coming quickly to her.

He took her in his arms and held her close enough to hear the beating of her heart. He spoke to her in low tones, and she put her fingers on his throat for the feel of the words. She nodded her head, smiling as she did so. She freed her hands from his embrace and used them to speak to him, almost unconsciously doing what she had done for many months past. He raised his hands and replied, his fingers moving more slowly than hers, but accurately.

She backed away from him in surprise, and the amazement on her face was great. In his eagerness to convey his meaning he went too fast and made a series of mistakes. She stared, then she started to smile, but the smile was not enough. She threw back her head and opened her mouth and laughed. The sound echoed across the lake. The thrushes seemed to catch it and weave it into their caroling. The lake seemed to catch it, for a succession of small ripples started to break against the stones along the shore. Danny caught it, for he joined in laughing with her.

"Come," he said, signing quickly the rest of his message that her parents and brothers were waiting for them at the house. "Come as my beloved. Will you, Melody?"

"Oh, Danny, you don't have to ask!"

"I know." His fingers moved quickly. "I think I've always known, but I want to hear you say it."

"I am your beloved, and you are mine." She smiled at him. "Does that make you happy?"

His only answer was to place a kiss on her lips, parted now that they might the more readily laugh again.

Then Melody thought of the apple parings and the way they had persistently fallen into the letter *D*. "Oh, Danny, I've always belonged to you–since the beginning of the world."

"And to its end," he said.

He linked his arm in hers and they walked down the road together, away from the green secrecy of the woods and the fluting of the thrushes to the house where the lamp had been lighted and dear ones were waiting for them.